SOUNDS
OF
SILENCE

PHILLIP TOMASSO

BARKING RAIN PRESS

Sounds of Silence

Copyright © 2013 Phillip Tomasso (www.philliptomoasso.com)

Edited by Dr. Julie Spergel

Barking Rain Press
PO Box 822674
Vancouver, WA 98682 USA
www.barkingrainpress.org

ISBN print: 1-935460-41-2
ISBN eBook: 1-935460-37-4
Library of Congress Control Number: 2013951284

First Edition: October 2013

Printed in the United States of America

9 7 8 1 9 3 5 4 6 0 4 4 1

DEDICATION

To Phillip, Grant, and Raeleigh,
I love you more than life itself.

This book is dedicated to the memory
of my dear friend, Todd Calabrese

SPECIAL THANKS TO:

Nisha L. (Ferry) Cerame, Director of Development
Joe Yonda, Psychologist
Rochester School for the Deaf

Harry G. Lang, Professor, Department of Research
National Technical Institute for the Deaf

Rochester Institute of Technology

Vivian Vande Velde, young adult author;
Dr. Julie Spergel, my editor;
Christine Wzros-Lucacci, Gregory Palmer,
Corrine Chorney, Marian Gowen, Max Wihite,
Ms. Lois Smiley and Steven DeBottis,
my ASL instructors;
and last, but not least, I thank God.

CHAPTER 1
END OF JUNE

I was sick and didn't know it. By the time I did, it was already too late. Patrick and I tossed a baseball back and forth in the backyard. He stood by the tree at one end of the yard. I aligned myself with a fern my mother had planted. We knew it was about the right distance from a pitcher to the catcher because we had practiced out here lots of times before.

As soon as my black lab, Whitney, knew she wasn't getting the ball, she hid from the sun under the shade of the maple tree. It was early evening, but still really hot.

We took it easy since we had a Little League game the next day and didn't want to wear ourselves out. Ever since T-ball days, we've managed to be on the same team. How lucky is that?

He is the catcher for the team. I'm one of the pitchers. I guess Batavia Little League coaches didn't like to split up a pitcher—catcher pair. It could be devastating, like separating twins or something.

"Hey, Marco? Did you get that new baseball video game?" Patrick asked.

I knew what he was talking about. The game was the latest, hottest on the market. "Yeah, I got it. It cost me a few weeks' worth of allowance, but it was worth it, I think. It's so real, it's like being at an actual game. Get this, you can even make the players spit!"

"No way."

"Oh yeah. It's awesome," I said. He threw the ball high, a simulated pop fly. I ran to get under it and caught it.

Had to close my eyes a second. My head hurt a little.

"You okay?"

I nodded. "The graphics are wild. The players look so real, it's like you're really there. The ump calls balls and strikes. There's an organ player charging

2 — PHILLIP TOMASSO

up the crowd between pitches and after the top and bottom of each inning. Players grunt when they're sliding into home. What can I say—it's awesome."

"That's what I figured." His eyes were wide and his tongue practically dangled from the corner of his mouth. I knew what he wanted.

"Wanna go play it?" I took in a deep breath, held it, and blew it out. Maybe I needed to rest. A video game would be easier than playing catch.

"Definitely. Let's go." He took off his mitt.

"Hey guys!" It was Jordan and Tyrone, two guys from Patrick's and my sixth-grade class. They leaned on the chainlink fence set around the backyard. For the first time, Tyrone was on the same baseball team as Patrick and me. He usually played first or second base.

Jordan's team was the coveted Joe's Collision Shop. The owner, Joe, had shirts made with his cool car wreck logo on the back.

Sally's House of Hair wound up sponsoring my team. Our logo was nothing fancier than a pair of scissors instead of a "Y" in the name Sally. *Yuck!* We made sure that when we talked about ourselves, we dropped the *Sally*. At least we didn't have to wear something like pink jerseys.

But it wasn't only the cool name and jerseys that made Joe's team seem better—it was their batting and fielding stats. They were a solid team, year after year.

Patrick and I strolled to the fence and fist-bumped Jordan and Tyrone. I wanted to get inside, get on the couch, rest my head. It looked like the video game would have to wait. "What's up?"

"Not much," Tyrone said. "Jordan's dad took us to the batting cages."

I tried not to look at Tyrone like he was some kind of traitor for hanging out with Jordan the night before a big game. The last thing our team needed was Tyrone telling Jordan, the opposition, about our strengths and weaknesses.

Sure, he and Jordan were good friends. They always hung out. Maybe it wasn't such a big deal. How could I blame Tyrone? I tried to look at it this way: at least he got in some batting practice. I mean, I liked going to the cages, too. Most ballplayers did. They were indoors so you didn't have to be at it when it was cold or rainy. What's not to like? "Cool," I said. "How'd you guys do?"

Tyrone shrugged. "I did all right, but Jordan was killing the balls. He missed, like, only five out of fifty pitches!"

"Nice going." I wasn't really glad to hear this; the coach had me pitching tomorrow's game, and now here was my teammate telling me about what a hot-hitter I'd be facing. But if Tyrone wasn't telling us how well Jordan had done, Jordan would have been telling us himself.

"Don't I know it!"

Sweat beaded on my forehead. Probably pre-game jitters. Too bad Jordan didn't play on our team. We could always use another hard-hitter. But he didn't. So now it became more important for us to win. If I didn't strike Jordan out, he'd never let me live it down.

"Wanna play catch?" Patrick asked.

I shot Patrick a look. Why would he ask them to play catch?

"Nah," Jordan said. "We're headed to my house."

"See you guys at practice tomorrow, before the game?" Tyrone asked.

"Get there early," I said. "I want to practice some new pitches I've been working on."

Jordan arched his eyebrows.

"Cool," Tyrone said, as they headed off. "See you guys then."

Patrick tossed me the ball.

"You got new pitches?"

"Nah. I just wanted to psych out Jordan a bit. Think it worked?"

"He looked scared to me."

We laughed and did our special handshake. It was quick. Three claps with our right hands, then an over-the-top, upside-down clap before putting our mitts back on. The video game was momentarily forgotten.

This time I sent the ball toward him like a rocket. The air whistled as it parted to let the ball pass. Then came the satisfying sound of the ball slamming into padded leather.

"That stung, man." Patrick shook off his mitt and rubbed his palm down the front of his jeans. "I thought we were just taking it easy, you know?"

"Sorry. I just, well, I guess Jordan got me worked up."

"Why?" He threw the ball back to me.

"Because he wanted me to know he went to the batting cages."

"You think he told you that to rattle you?"

"Yep. I sure do." I sent the ball back to Patrick—hard.

"He knows you're pitching tomorrow?"

"He's with Tyrone, right? I'm sure Tyrone told him." It didn't matter. Jordan would have found out at the game tomorrow. But knowing in advance gave him the chance to stop by and make me nervous—or at least *try* to make me nervous.

"Ah, so what," Patrick said.

"He's a good hitter."

"And you're a good pitcher. You got nothing to worry about, and if you pitch like this tomorrow, Jordan won't be hitting a thing."

I smiled at the thought of him striking out. "If he was smacking them at the cages . . ."

"Forget it. He was probably in the slow-pitch cage. Who couldn't hit a ball floating at him like a butterfly? Your arm is like a gun. The ball is a bullet. He'll be swinging at shadows tomorrow."

"You mean that?"

"You know it."

Mom pushed the kitchen window open. "Marco?"

I rolled my eyes as I turned to face her. She was always hovering over me, treating me like a baby. I know it's what mothers do, but Dad was never this annoying.

"Yeah, Ma?"

"Patrick's mom just called. She has to work late again and asked if it was all right that he stay for dinner."

I looked at Patrick. He didn't look happy. His mother worked a lot and he only saw his father every other weekend. "Awesome, you can eat with us!" I almost added "again," but stopped myself just in time.

"You know it." He smiled, though it looked somewhat forced. At least it was a smile.

"It's okay with me. I already told her it wasn't a problem," she said. "Dinner's just about ready here. Why don't you two come in and get washed up?" She closed the window.

"All right," I shouted. We ran together and slapped high-fives. "Hey, wanna play the video game right after dinner?"

"Perfect!" he said.

"I'm hungry." I patted my belly.

"Me, too." He smiled. "Race ya!"

We ran at the house like hungry cheetahs chasing after prey, Whitney right beside us, her tail wagging, knowing that she was also about to get some chow.

Patrick won. I had to stop. Running made my head feel like it might fall right off my shoulders.

CHAPTER 2

Intense was not a strong enough word to describe the pressure I felt. We were one hard-fought run ahead and it was the end of the game. Joe's Collision Shop was up to bat with two outs, but their runner on first had just stolen second.

Jordan dug in at the plate with three balls and one strike against him.

As I stood on the pitcher's mound, I imagined myself to be Hoyt Wilhelm, the first-ever relief pitcher introduced into the Hall of Fame in 1985, a player my grandpa was always talking about. I might only be twelve, but I bet I knew more about Wilhelm and his career—thanks to grandpa—than any grownup who claimed to be a baseball fan.

This was something I often did when in tight spots. Pretending to be Wilhelm, who pitched in over a thousand games during his twenty-one-year career, helped me focus through the taunts of the Collisions, the yells from the packed bleachers, and the pounding ache in my head that had started at the top of the third inning.

Jordan backed away from the plate, giving me a moment to massage the painful cramp in the back of my neck and consider the best pitch to throw. He didn't seem nervous. Why would he be? The count was in his favor. Instead, he took a few practice swings and then tapped the end of the bat against his cleats. Stepping back up to the plate, he settled into a perfect stance—legs shoulder-width apart, elbow up, and head in. He looked as eager for the next pitch as I was anxious to throw it.

Behind me, over my right shoulder, the guy on second base bounced up and down smugly as if ready to steal third.

I tucked my head down so the bill of my cap shielded my eyes from the sunlight. I'd pitched many games under the sun, but it had never bothered me so much before. Today, the bright light was more than annoying—it felt painful, making the back of my eyes throb.

There was nothing I could do to protect my body from the sun's heat. Instead, the sweat seemed to spill from my pores, especially where the baseball cap touched my forehead. Salty drops stung my eyes. I shook my head, trying to concentrate.

With my mitt up to my face so Jordan could not see anything, I let my right hand caress the ball inside my glove. My fingers cradled the ball in a variety of pitching holds. I had practiced the holds Coach had taught me, getting my fingers used to some of the odd grips.

Squatting behind the plate, Patrick signaled the next pitch by pointing two fingers to the ground. A curve. I shook my head. Last time I'd thrown a curve, Jordan hit a double. It wasn't that Jordan was great at hitting curves, it was more that I wasn't all that good at throwing one correctly. I was pretty good at a few different pitches, but the curve was one I was still practicing with my dad.

My fingers massaged the ball's stitching the way an animal lover might pet the silky, furry skin behind a dog's ear. This relaxed me.

Patrick suggested another pitch, a screwball—where the ball spins kind of weird so it goes up and down and is very unpredictable. If I couldn't throw a solid curve, there'd be no way I'd risk a screwball. I didn't want to end up walking Jordan. That would be as bad as his hitting another double.

I shook my head again. I knew what I wanted.

When Patrick pointed one finger to the ground, then slapped the inside of his thigh, I nodded in agreement—a fastball change-up. Dad and I had spent hours in the yard practicing this one.

All I could hear were the cheers and jeers from the people in the bleachers. Normally, spectators yelling my name was like music to my ears. Normally, imagining I was Wilhelm playing in a major league stadium in the last inning of the last game of the World Series made the game that much more exciting.

Now I just wanted to get this over with.

I needed to get to the cooling shade of our little wooden dugout, but forced myself not to rush. I glanced over my shoulder. The runner on second was leading, ready to make a break for third. I could throw the ball to Tyrone, on second, and hope he'd be able to tag the runner out.

But that might backfire. The runner might sprint for third and make it. We couldn't afford a runner on third, not with a batter who could hit a homerun on the right throw—or on the wrong one, depending on your point of view. I took a deep breath to steady myself.

I let the ball sit deep in my palm. I wound up and, at the last second, just before releasing the ball, lifted my top two fingers off of it.

My pitch sped toward the catcher's mitt. Just as Jordan swung with enough power to knock the ball out of the park, it jumped slightly upward. His bat missed. The ball slammed into Patrick's mitt with a loud *whumph-pop!*

Strike two.

Cheers erupted. Clapping. Whistling. My heart beat so fast I feared I might pass out.

I took another deep breath and glanced at the bleachers along the first base line where my mom, dad and eight-year-old sister, Marie, sat. They waved to me. My father cupped his hands around his mouth. "One more, Marco! Throw it right to Patrick! That's it, just one more!"

Three balls. Two strikes. Full count.

Stay calm. Concentrate. I breathed in, held it a moment, and breathed out in a long sigh.

I signaled the next pitch by touching the brim of my cap with the ball. Patrick nodded. Fastball. Anything else would be risky. A knuckle ball would be nice, but they're hard to throw—and harder to catch. If I threw a wild ball, the guy on second would steal third and maybe home, tying up the game.

A fastball definitely made the most sense.

I wound up, released the ball, and watched it whiz through the air. Jordan swung.

For a brief moment I thought I saw the bat connect, and thought I heard the smack of impact. My heart raced, though, as I realized what had actually happened.

The sound I had heard was the ball colliding with Patrick's mitt and the swoosh of the swinging bat as it cut through empty air.

Strike three.

I jumped up and down on the pitcher's mound in tempo with Patrick's gangly leaps, but had to stop. Fast. Jumping made my head feel as though my brain was about to slosh out through my eye sockets. I tried to stand still, but could feel myself swaying slightly as my teammates rushed the mound. "Way to go, Marco!"

Jordan headed back to the bench with the rest of his team. He wasn't looking our way. He just stared at the dirt.

The guys were slapping my back and sloppily rubbing the top of my baseball cap to congratulate me. Every slap, pat, and nudge shot straight to my pounding head.

"Great pitching, Marco!" The coach wrapped an arm around my shoulder.

"Thanks." I tried to smile, but my body suddenly felt very hot, like I might burst into flames.

"Marco?"

I nodded—just a little nod—because my head might fall off. As I focused on his face, my legs gave out. My vision blurred. The coach's face seemed to snap backwards. I looked toward the ground and before I could say anything, the grass rushed up to meet my face.

For a split second I saw the cleats of people around me. Then everything went dark.

CHAPTER 3

Patrick shook my shoulder as I struggled to open my eyes. "Marco! Marco! What's wrong?" I waved a hand to fend him off—his voice was so loud! My stomach roiled, and I just knew everyone would watch me get sick.

"Get away!" I sort of rolled onto my side and the muscles in my shoulders and arms went rigid as my stomach heaved. My throat burned and my head pounded. Sunlight barbequed my eyeballs, so I slapped my lids over them and concentrated on catching my breath.

When I opened them again Dad and Mom were kneeling by my side. Mom massaged my back. "You think you're done, Marco?"

I nodded. "I'm okay."

Mom touched my forehead. "He's really hot."

They helped me to my feet. Mom held one arm, Dad the other. We walked toward the car. I kept my head down and eyes shut. I couldn't do much but stumble along. My toes dragged across the dirt and grass of the field, and then over loose parking lot gravel.

Dad snapped the button on the car key and clicked the locks on the car doors. "I'll start the engine and get the air conditioning going."

"No, Dad, no. I'm cold." My lips quivered and teeth chattered. The flesh along my arms was covered with goose bumps.

"Cold?" Mom repeated in surprise.

"Does that mean we've got to ride with the air off?" Marie whined. "It's like a hundred degrees out. Two hundred inside the car."

"Get in the car, Marie," Dad said. "Roll your window down if you'd like."

Dad's voice was tinged with annoyance. If I didn't feel so sick, I'd have given her my best sure-to-infuriate grin.

"Good. That will at least get rid of the puke smell coming from Marco." Marie folded her arms.

"Ride up front next to your father. I'll ride in back with Marco."

I didn't care who rode where. I was just thankful to be in the car and not down on my hands and knees, vomiting while half the town watched.

Dad eased the car out of the lot. Everyone was quiet for a while. Thank heaven for the silence.

Mom slipped an arm around my shoulders. "How are you?"

I didn't usually like it when Mom worried about how I was feeling, but now her arm around me felt good. Real good. My head hurt. My entire body ached. Keeping my eyes open seemed impossible; even with my eyes closed, the light seemed too bright. "The light hurts my eyes."

"There's no light on," Dad said. "Is sunlight coming in through the windows?"

"Some." Mom's reply sounded weak. "Marco, honey, what else doesn't feel well?"

"All of me. I got a pretty bad headache during the game, but I thought it was because I was excited. But now, now I feel like I have the flu. Everything hurts. And I'm so cold." I couldn't stop shivering.

"I'm calling the doctor." Mom rooted around in her purse, probably searching for her cell phone.

"Oh great," Marie groaned. "That's what I need, a flu at the beginning of summer."

"Marie," Dad warned. "Stop it."

My mother gently touched my face. "Marco? Marco?"

"Huh?"

"You fell asleep on me. Stay awake, all right? Stay with me." Mom's voice shifted from concern to demanding as she spoke into the phone. "Hello? Yes. This is Mrs. Lippa, Marco's mother. I need to speak to Dr.—absolutely not! Don't put me on hold. I need to speak to Dr. Davis now. This is an emergency."

I couldn't believe how horrible I felt. Ten minutes ago, I'd been part of a winning baseball team, ready to go for ice cream and celebrate with my friends. Now all I could think about was getting home, getting under a blanket, and having Mom and Dad wait on me.

"We were at my son's baseball game and he threw up. He says his head hurts. I haven't taken his temperature." Mom touched my forehead again. "Each time I feel his head, though, he's hotter. Right now it feels like he's burning up." After a few moments of silence, Mom added, "Yes, right, the light bothers his eyes and he seems lethargic."

Lethargic. I'd heard the word before. What did it mean?

"Dr. Davis wants us to meet him at the hospital," Mom reported to Dad as she snapped her phone shut.

The word "hospital" should have been enough to have me bolting upright in my seat, but lead weighted my eyelids and it didn't seem worth the battle to force them open. Nothing seemed worth the battle.

"Hospital? Mom, what's wrong with Marco?" Marie wailed as dark silence settled around me.

෬෬

My eyelids fluttered open. Dad had me by the arms and was pulling me out of the car.

"Dad?" My throat felt dry and my back felt bruised, as if Marie had been kicking me for an hour. I wasn't even sure I could stand. "Dad, I don't feel well."

"I know, Marco. Don't worry." He breathed heavily as he lifted me into his arms. My legs dangled over one side of him, my head hung painfully over the other. Then Dad was running with me, and my head wobbled and bounced.

"I have to throw up."

He stopped, set me down on my knees, and placed his hand on my back. "Hang in there, buddy."

The doors swooshed open. Mom and Marie ran toward me. A tall black man dressed in white followed behind them, pushing a wheelchair.

"Let's get him into the chair," the man said. He and my father lifted me up and eased me into the wheelchair.

My family ran alongside as the man wheeled me back through automated doors and into the emergency room.

"Mom?" The acid taste in my mouth, mixed with my saliva, dribbled down my chin. I used the back of my wrist to wipe it away. "Mom?"

"I'm right here." She took my hand and it felt good to have her hold it, like she could protect me.

"We're going to take him back," said the man who'd wheeled me in. "Only one of you can go with him."

She knelt down next to me. "Do you want me or Dad to go with you?"

As a sort-of answer, I turned to my mom and asked: "What's wrong with me?" I thought I might cry, but tried to hold back the tears. I had never felt so awful, so cold; I thought I might be dying.

"You go with him," Dad said. I couldn't see his face, but he sounded worried.

"Marco," Marie said weakly. Tears streamed down her cheeks. I managed half a smile before the man pushed the wheelchair through a set of doors.

Everything spun out of whack. Colors blended. Two men lifted me onto a bed and between cold sheets. A woman in baby-blue pajamas jabbed a needle into the top of my hand. I screamed.

Someone held my hand. Mom stood by my side.

"I can't keep my eyes open." My stomach flip-flopped. I might get sick again. My dry mouth demanded water.

"Stay awake, honey. I don't know if you should go to sleep."

I wasn't sure I had a choice.

CHAPTER 4

I knew I was in the hospital, but everything felt like some bizarre and twisted dream. I felt hot. Then cold. Then hot again. My body ached—all of my joints, my neck, my head. And whatever didn't ache, burned.

Whenever I opened my eyes, I saw shadowy faces hovering over me. Sometimes it was Mom and Dad, sometimes Marie. Maybe other times doctors and nurses. It was when I opened my eyes and saw no one, just the room, dark, that I felt alone and frightened.

One word kept coming into my mind. I'd heard people around me saying it, sometimes loudly, mostly in whispers. Meningitis.

At times the dream turned into a nightmare. Monsters would attack, biting and stinging my arms. Once, while I was curled into a ball, I was stung down at the bottom of my back, close to my rear end. The pain shot through my body like fire racing through my spine.

Most of the time, my body felt drained, as if all my blood had been sucked out and all that was left were heavy bones under wrinkled, sagging skin.

When I opened my eyes, the sun poured through the window into my hospital room. Flowers, balloons, and fruit baskets sat clustered together on the table. Mom was sleeping in the chair by the window. Had she spent the night?

"Mom?"

Something felt strange. I couldn't hear the sound of my voice. My heart beat hard inside my ribcage. "Mom?" I said again. No. I heard nothing.

Had I talked to anyone since I arrived at the hospital? I wasn't sure—it was all so hazy. I felt tired and weak. My dry and scratchy throat felt rusty from neglect. Maybe I was still asleep, still dreaming.

I tried again. "Mom? Mom, can you hear me? Ma?"

She woke with a start and jumped up. Her pillow fell to the floor. She rushed over to my bed. I could see her lips move. She smiled, cried silently, ran her fingers through my hair.

She thought I could hear. She had no idea I was clueless about what she said.

I poked a finger in each ear in search of cotton balls, or earplugs, in search of whatever had plugged them up, but found nothing. If I hadn't been so exhausted, I would have laughed. What was going on?

"Mom?" It was a test. I knew I was talking; I could feel the vibration in my throat and jaw.

Silence.

She backed away from the bed, as if something frightened her. Her lips kept moving, faster now. Her eyes got wide while the rest of her face crinkled up, the way she looked when she saw a spider on the kitchen countertop, but I still couldn't hear a word she said.

"I can't hear. I can't hear you." I tried to sit up, but dizziness settled me back against the pillows. "Mom!" I was about to fall out of bed. I grabbed the railing and clamped it with a white-knuckled grip.

She looked panicked and started snapping fingers near my face. I just kept shaking my head. "I can't hear it."

She ran toward the door and darted out into the hall.

All this activity was like watching television with the sound off. Where was the remote? I needed to turn the volume up, but there was nothing to reach for or to press.

Whenever I swam underwater, my ears would fill up, and all I had to do was rattle my head from side to side to clear them and everything would be all right. I slapped at the sides of my head, attempting to shake out whatever it was that was keeping me from hearing. I was still doing this when my mother returned, dragging a doctor along by the sleeve of her white coat.

CHAPTER 5

I wanted to get up because it seemed like I couldn't. I tried pulling myself into a sitting position. My head felt like a bucket filled halfway to the top with water that sloshed around inside my skull, knocking me off balance.

I fell back against the pillow. My head throbbed. Lifting my arm felt like trying to lift up the back end of a car. The room seemed to spin.

I closed my eyes. Opened them. Mom looked at me. I looked away. She probably thought I was going to fall out of bed, despite the bed rails. That's how I felt. A baby bird perched at the edge of a nest a hundred feet off the ground.

I just wanted to get better and get out of there.

Mom walked over to the bed. Her lips moved but I heard nothing—not the squeak of her chair, not her steps, not her words.

Suddenly, the head of the bed rose up into a sitting position. For a moment I thought she must have spoken a magic spell, and I looked at her in awe. Then she showed me a white remote control connected to the bed. She pointed at the button she'd pressed. There were four, each clearly labeled. Head up. Head down. Legs up. Legs down. She set the remote next to my hand.

My cheeks felt hot, as if I were standing too close to a campfire.

The doctor on the opposite side of the bed wore a nameplate, Dr. Green. She was tall and thin with a friendly expression. Her hair was a mess and part of her shirt was not tucked in. This was the woman who was going to take care of me? She didn't look like she could take care of herself.

Dr. Green waved, smiled. She got up close to my face. All the while her lips moved, her smile never wilted.

I shook my head. "I can't hear you. I can't hear a thing." Not hearing my own voice was weird.

Dr. Green's smile only widened as she fitted a cone-shaped piece onto her little flashlight-thingy and looked in both my ears. At least now she'd see the junk, or gunk, or whatever it was in there and clear it out. Things would be back to normal in no time.

I was thinking I should call Patrick when I got home. He must have talked with Tyrone or Jordan by now. He'd know if anyone had anything to say about my pitching.

Mom gripped my right hand in both of hers while she talked to Dr. Green, who was watching her expectantly. I sure hoped my mom was asking the big question: *Why can't my son hear?*

Dr. Green kept nodding her head and glancing at me with a smile. I tapped the bed, frustrated at being left out of the conversation. Did she think smiling at me would make me think everything was fine? I couldn't hear a thing.

That didn't feel so fine.

What had she seen when she looked in my ears? Why wasn't she using a pair of tweezers or something to pull out whatever was stuck in there? "What is it?" I asked.

Mom looked at me wide-eyed and stiff-smiled. Cardboard-like. She looked afraid.

"Mom, what's going on?" I had to close my eyes and take a breath to calm the churning in my stomach. This would all be over soon. This would all be over soon.

My mother's lips moved very slowly, exaggerating. You'll be okay. But her eyes were wet, and her expression was sad. It didn't look as though she believed what she had just told me.

So if she didn't, how could I?

⚭

With Mom pushing me from behind, I sat in the wheelchair and cradled my stomach.

Mom had written me a note that Dr. Green arranged for an ear specialist to see me right away. With my brain still swimming around my skull, I was on some wild ride at an amusement park, instead of just rolling down the hospital corridor. We entered the ear specialist's office.

The doctor, Dr. Allen, came right over and shook hands with me first, then with Mom. Unlike Dr. Green, his hair was combed and his shirt was tucked in. His office had a desk, a couch, and some art on the walls. Everything looked neat and in place.

Dr. Allen held a clipboard and a pad of paper. He wrote on the pad for a while before showing it to me. *Marco, you will take tests. You will wear headphones and sit across from me while I operate a machine—turning dials and pressing buttons. When you hear anything in your right ear, raise your right hand. Do the same thing for the left ear and hand. OK?*

I handed the note to Mom and shrugged. I'd done these tests before. No big deal.

He led us into another room, twice the size of his office. Computers, printers, and other equipment took up space everywhere, with lights blinking on and off all over the place.

After I settled a big set of headphones over my ears, Dr. Allen spun dials and pressed buttons on a machine by his desk. Try as I might, I couldn't hear a thing. Not the beeping I'd expected. Maybe static in my right ear? I wasn't sure, but I raised my hand just in case. A faint hissing in my left ear had me raising my hand again.

"I hear static," I said. "It's in both ears. It comes and goes. Is that what I'm supposed to be listening for?"

The doctor smiled and pointed to the pad of paper. *Listen for high and low-pitched sounds.*

So hearing static was wrong? There were no high or low-pitched sounds… well, not that I could hear. At least I heard static. That had to count for something. Maybe once the static cleared, I'd be able to hear again.

This test lasted a few more minutes. When it ended, I looked over at my mother, who never blinked as she watched the doctor write things down.

Once I took off the headset, I could still hear the static. I stuck a finger in my ear and swirled it around, trying to unclog whatever mess was in there. It didn't help.

Then Dr. Allen smiled and tapped a finger on what he'd written down. *Bone conductor test. It transmits sound through bone by vibration. You won't feel the vibrations. When you hear something in either ear, raise your hand.*

He put an earphone in each of my ears, and a headband around my forehead. Then he gave me a thumbs-up, raising his eyebrows as if asking me if I was ready to begin.

I smiled back at him. "Ready."

After the test was over, the doctor again wrote something on his clipboard. Then he wrote on the pad and handed it to me. *Next, we'll test speech.*

This didn't make sense. As best I could tell, I talked fine. Or maybe I didn't? Was I slurring my words? "Am I talking funny?"

Mom squeezed my hand.

Dr. Allen shook his head, and wrote: *No. We are not testing YOUR speech. We are testing to see if you can hear others talk. I will say a two-syllable word into a microphone. You don't have to say a thing, OK?*

I sat with my eyes closed for a while, trying to hear something. "When is the test going to begin?" I finally asked, opening my eyes.

I watched as the doctor wrote on his clipboard. Then he wrote on the pad of paper and showed it to me. *Done.*

He nodded his head and smiled. If that smile was meant to comfort me, it didn't. I was confused. Had he said things that I didn't hear, and the test was now over? I couldn't help feeling like I'd just failed miserably.

Dr. Allen came over and patted me on the back. He knelt down in front of me, still smiling and nodding. He held up a thin instrument with a round, foamy end that reminded me of a sucker, and showed his pad of paper to me.

This is a probe. It goes in the ear. Let me know if you hear anything. (I'll be increasing and decreasing air pressure.)

I shrugged. *Whatever.* Increasing and decreasing air pressure? Like that meant anything to me. I sat where I was as the doctor typed away at his keyboard. He would look up at me, then go back to typing. Look up. Go back to typing.

The printer by a computer spat out a series of graphs on several connected sheets of paper. I watched it, still listening—waiting for whatever increased and decreased air pressure might sound like—wondering what all of this meant.

When all the testing finally ended, Dr. Allen said something to Mom, then wrote on his pad. *We'll be right back.*

I watched them leave the room, trying to smile, but this was ridiculous. Who was I kidding? I had not heard a single sound during any of the tests, except for the static which kept coming and going whether I had a headset on or not.

What did that mean?

How long was this going to last?

I could handle not hearing for a week or two. But summer had just started. Baseball was just getting going. No *way* was I spending the whole summer this way!

That would stink.

That would really suck.

CHAPTER 6

Alone in Dr. Allen's office, I stood up, sat down, rested my chin on my knuckles, and leaned my head back against the wall. Boredom would have been better than how nervous I felt. My stomach churned. I thought I might throw up again.

I rubbed my belly gently, hoping to calm myself down, and looked around.

Dr. Allen's office seemed dark. The desk was made of a dark wood and the bookcases that edged the walls were of a similar dark wood. His flat-screen computer monitor was black, his penholder was black, and the leather chair behind the desk was black. Even the black-and-white framed photos of waterfalls were carefully placed on white walls.

Books of various sizes lined the shelf behind me. I couldn't pronounce more than half the titles.

Whatever was going on had to be serious. They'd left me in the office for more than half an hour. I tried to ignore how frightened I felt. It was like that fear you have when you're little and lying alone in your room at night and you just know there's a monster under your bed. You figure if you don't move—don't even breathe—then it won't get you.

Nothing made any sense. There had to be a reason I couldn't hear. Once they figured out what was broken, they'd fix it. After all, that was what doctors did. They cured sick people. How long would it be before they'd get around to fixing me?

Then I remembered Tommy.

He used to live in the house next door. A hornet had climbed into his ear, stung him repeatedly as it crawled deeper and deeper inside. When he got back from the hospital, he had a bandage on his ear. I asked him to play outside. He said he wanted to stay inside. He pushed open the door, and as he looked over my shoulder, he hurried me inside his house, like he thought a swarm of bees were waiting to attack. In his room, he told me how insanely painful the stings had been, and about how the doctors had to remove the hornet. Days passed before he came out to play again. Days!

I didn't feel any pain. But something was wrong with my ears. Something must be wrong. I just wanted the doctors to fix it, like they did for my friend.

The door to the doctor's office finally opened. Mom and Dad walked in, followed by Dr. Allen. He was smiling, but his face looked pretty stiff to me. Mom's eyes were red and she was biting her upper lip.

"Dad, why am I here?" I tugged at my earlobe. I could feel my throat vibrate and the static was back, a little louder than before. I kept coming back to the same hope: if the doctors got rid of the static, maybe I'd be able to hear again.

Dad stared at me. Only his eyes moved, like he was watching me from behind almond shaped cut-outs in one of those store-bought plastic Halloween masks.

Mom took my hand, sitting in the chair next to where I stood. My legs felt weak, my knees wobbled. I sat back down. Dad came over and stood behind me. He put his hands on my shoulders. The doctor moved around the desk and plopped into that big black leather chair. The air in the room seemed thicker, making it hard to breathe.

Questions kept forming in my mind, but I didn't seem capable of asking them. And maybe, I don't know, I wasn't really thinking I would like the answers I would… hear.

Dr. Davis wrote on his tablet: *You had meningitis.*

I raised my eyebrows and shook my head as if saying: Yeah? And what is that? I didn't really know what had made me sick. It had felt like a pretty bad flu. All I could really recall was passing out after the baseball game. I only vaguely remembered riding in the car to the hospital, and then the nurses and doctors rushing to get me to a bed in the emergency room.

He handed my parents and me a few stapled pages. At the top of the first page I saw the words: "Center for Disease Control and Prevention website." In capital letters it said, "What Is Meningitis?" I started to read:

Bacterial Meningitis: an infection of the fluid of a person's spinal cord and the fluid that surrounds the brain, can be severe and may result in brain damage, hearing loss, learning disability, or death…

My heart beat fast. "Am I going to die?"

Dr. Allen shook his head and smiled. I was really starting to hate all the smiling these doctors did.

I pressed my tongue against my top back teeth and tried to swallow. There was no spit in my mouth. I wiped sweat off my forehead and pointed at the words "hearing loss" in the handout.

Dr. Allen pursed his lips and nodded.

This couldn't be happening. I pointed to the words "brain damage."

The doctor shook his head.

How could he be so sure? Had anyone tested me for that? "How do you know I had meningitis?"

Dr. Allen turned a page in my handout and pointed to the top. I read the first paragraph under the heading "Signs and Symptoms of Meningitis."

High fever, headache, and a stiff neck are common symptoms of meningitis. Other symptoms may include nausea, vomiting, discomfort looking into bright lights…

I thought back to the way I felt the night before and during the baseball game. That was exactly what I'd felt. *Exactly.*

Dr. Allen wrote on his pad. *You were in a coma for eight days.*

"I was asleep for more than a week?" I felt the air being sucked out of my lungs. "I've been in the hospital that long?" It seemed like the game was only yesterday. *Wasn't it?*

Mom put a hand on my leg. Dad, still standing behind me, rubbed my shoulders. I felt alone in the room.

"Did I almost die?"

Dr. Allen paused before nodding.

"How come I got sick?" I felt suddenly tired as I read the answer. *It could have been spread from a cough or a kiss. Some people carry the bacteria around and never get sick, but manage to infect the people they come in contact with.*

"Was I contagious? Am I contagious now?"

Dr. Allen nodded, then wrote again on his pad and handed it to me. *You were contagious. Not now. Everyone on your team, even the coaches, needed to go to the hospital. They all got checked out, and some were given antibiotics. Of course, your dad, mom, and sister were examined, too. If this had happened during the school year, everyone in your class, even your teachers, might have needed treatment. The school would have had to scrub down your locker, desks and destroy textbooks. Meningitis is a serious illness.*

"But I'm better now, right? I mean, I'm not still sick, am I? Am I going to get sicker? Am I going to hear again?" I kept talking. I wanted to stop, to give the doctor a chance to answer, but couldn't; I was a little out of control. "I'll hear again. Right? Dad? Mom?" I looked at one, then the other.

Mom gave my leg a squeeze as if trying to reassure me, while Dr. Allen wrote on his pad for several more moments. When he handed the paper to me, I didn't feel like reading his answer. I wanted Dr. Allen to talk, and me to listen. That was what I wanted.

You're not still sick, and I see no reason why you would get sick again. You are a very fortunate young man. Some people who contract meningitis do not survive. Let me review some of the results from your hearing tests, OK?

"I don't care about reviewing the tests." I might have been yelling. It felt like I was yelling. I wanted to be yelling. "I just need to know what happened to my hearing!"

Dr. Allen wrote on his pad again and handed it to me. Then he said something to my parents. Mom looked like she'd placed something in her mouth before realizing it was a red-hot chili pepper. Her eyes opened wider, her nostrils flared, and her lips looked glued together. I read what the doctor wrote.

Meningitis gave you a very high fever, and the fever destroyed something called fine hair cells in your ears. These fine hair cells are what allow you to hear.

I struggled to catch my breath, to keep my cool. I wasn't going to cry—not here. Not now. "What's that mean? Does that mean I'm deaf, that I'm going to stay this way?"

For just a moment, Dr. Allen looked like he'd also placed a piece of that chili pepper in his mouth, but then his face went flat. No smile. No wide eyes. And he nodded.

"But that can't be. I hear things. I can hear static. It comes and goes, but I hear it," I explained, pointing at my ears. "Maybe once that clears up, I'll be able to hear again?"

My parents' eyes brightened and were hopeful, like mine, as we waited. That static I heard—it had to mean something!

The doctor's chest rose and fell in a heavy sigh. He wrote on his pad: *What you are describing is called tinnitus, a ringing in the ears. We don't know why this happens, what causes it, or how to stop it.*

Stop it? Why would I want to do that? It was sound—it proved I could still hear! "So I'll be able to hear again, I mean, once the static stops." It wasn't a question. I was telling the doctor what had to happen.

That static sound may never stop. But if it does, it does not necessarily mean that you will be able to hear again.

The static sound may never stop? This was insane! I wouldn't be able to take it. I was in a dream, no—a nightmare. Everything moved in slow motion. Like trying to get away from a dream-monster, only when you look down you see that your feet are on some kind of sticky floor—it gets harder and harder to take a step forward as the dream-monster closes in. And even though you realize it is a dream, it seems so real that you're terrified.

That's what was going on now. I was dreaming. Having this bizarre nightmare. There is nothing to be afraid of. All I have to do is scream, and I will wake myself up.

"Those hairs in my ear, they'll grow back, right? And when they do, I'll be able to hear again."

The hairs will not grow back.

I looked up, mouth open—no air in my lungs.

Dr. Allen looked away.

This is it, the part where the monster has it in for me. So I screamed.

CHAPTER 7

 sat on the mattress, my legs dangling over the edge, and waited for the physical therapist to show.

After being wheeled back from Dr. Allen's the day before, I had tried to walk to the bathroom. In the short distance from the chair to the toilet, my head became heavy and my vision blurred. Even though I'd leaned on the wall for support, my knees shook and I fell into the bathroom. All last night and this morning, when I wanted to go to the bathroom, my mom insisted on helping me.

"Where's Dad?" I asked. Mom stood by my bed.

She picked up the pad of paper we now kept by the hospital bed. She wrote something, and handed it over. *Work. He wants to be here, but can't.*

I nodded, acting like I understood. I mean I did, but I also wanted him with me. Dad built things in a factory. He used to work at this other, bigger company where he had an office and a secretary. He was a manager. The company didn't do so hot and had to let thousands and thousands of people go. Dad was one of them.

For a long time, he was home with us because he couldn't find a job. He eventually took this one at this factory where they make parts for air conditioners. I'd heard him and my mother talking about how he was forced to work twice as hard for less than half of what he used to earn.

He didn't talk much about the job and I could see a difference in him. At the old job, he'd come home from work smiling and talking. Now, he came home without much to say about anything. I knew why he did it. For us. I never heard him complain. And that was for Marie's and my sake, too.

Gift baskets lined the windowsill. Some came while I'd been in the coma. Some came yesterday. Mom told me Patrick and his mom had been up to see me a few times, but were advised to stay in the waiting area. I guess at some point after my fever broke, I was no longer contagious.

Today, Marie was finally allowed to visit. She walked around the room, but didn't pay much attention to me. She stopped in front of a fruit basket, took out a large orange, held it up, as if asking whether or not she could eat it.

I shrugged. She gently tapped a blue helium "Get Well Soon" balloon. It bobbed and swayed on its ribbon string. "Want that?"

She nodded vigorously.

"It's yours."

She untied the ribbon and then sat on the edge of my bed, and Mom peeled the orange for her.

"When can other people come visit me?" It seemed a shame that watching my mother peel an orange was suddenly the highlight of my day. Mom set the orange down on a piece of paper towel, and wrote: *Patrick called a few times, and so did some other boys from the team. Your coach called, and your grandparents...*

I shook my head. "That's not what I said. When can other people come visit me? It's because of how sick I was, isn't it? They're all afraid of me now. They think they will get sick and become deaf, don't they?"

My mother shook her head, but I knew I was right.

"Yeah, that's why no one has been here to see me except you, Marie, and Dad. And not even Dad."

Your father had to work. We can't afford to have him lose this job.

"You don't have to pay for me being here, do you?"

Her pen touched paper, but took some time before it wrote anything. *Some of it.*

She looked up. A woman entered. She smiled brightly, showing off gleaming white teeth, and waved hello. She took the pad from my mother. *Hello, Marco. I'm Melody. I'm going to help you work on your balance. How are you?*

"Me? I'm doing wonderful, just wonderful." I didn't hear the sarcasm in my reply, but knew it worked when my mother shot me a now-you-be-polite look.

Melody ignored my tone and wrote another note. *Let's take a walk.*

I wasn't anxious to try walking on my own. As if my anxiety were printed on my face, Melody smiled again. She held onto my hand and shoulder, guided me off the edge of the bed, and pulled me into a standing position.

My knees shook. I wasn't sure if I had enough energy to lift a leg in order to take a step. I knew that if I closed my eyes, I'd be asleep standing up.

When I thought I had my balance, I tried a step and was startled when Melody grabbed my shoulders. "I was about to fall, huh?"

She nodded and guided me back to the bed. Then she stepped out into the hallway and returned a moment later holding a cane.

I lowered my eyes and shook my head. This *couldn't* be happening.

Melody showed me the tablet. On it she had written: *Use this for now.*

"Will I always need it?" I asked.

She wrote again. *Too soon to tell.*

What kind of answer was that? I leaned on the cane and stood up. Then I took a step with my right leg and slid the cane forward in my right hand. I swayed to the left, and started to fall. I dropped the cane and reached for Melody.

She took hold of me and eased me back down onto the bed. Marie watched with her mouth frozen in an "O" shape. I could tell that her big brother being so helpless scared her.

Melody picked up the cane in her right hand and looked at me. She shook it in her right hand, then lifted and shook her left leg. She put both the cane and her left leg out in front of her. Then she brought her right leg forward to take another step.

She did this a few times before looking over at me as if to say, "Get it?" I nodded. Melody handed me the cane.

Mom nodded at me encouragingly. I focused on the cane in my right hand, took a step with my left leg and the cane, and then brought my right foot forward after that. I didn't fall.

So far, so good.

I should have felt better, but didn't. The cane might improve my gait, but I wanted to walk without it.

Melody and I inched down the hospital hallway.

Almost all of the hospital rooms had people in them. As I passed by each one, I couldn't help but look in. Mostly all I saw was the feet of beds—sheets over the legs of patients. The hall was pretty crowded with nurses, visitors, and sick people in plain, light-blue gowns like mine.

At the end of the hall, along a wall of wheelchairs, I saw Dr. Allen. He recognized me; I saw it in his face. His eyes opened wider, and his eyebrows arched up like an upside-down V. Maybe he was surprised to see me walking already. He waved hello.

The therapist handed him the pad of paper she had brought with her from my room. Dr. Allen wrote for a moment and then held the pad up so I could read what he'd written. *Just coming to see you. I brought you some information on the ear. Thought you might be interested.*

He handed Melody some papers. She flipped through them, showing each page to me. One was a full-color illustration of the inside of an ear.

"Dr. Allen, thank you, but I'm not really interested in the ear. You already told me everything I need to know. I'm going to stay deaf, and now I need to use a cane to walk."

Then, using the cane, I stomped away. I wanted to exaggerate a limp to illustrate my sarcasm, but when I leaned on the stick—balance became a priority. I didn't look back to see his expression, or to see if Melody was following me.

⌒∞⌒

I lay in bed, hot and sweaty, keeping my eyes closed. As hard as I could, I imagined I was at home in my room with my baseball posters on the walls, iPod in its docking station, Nintendo DS lying on the floor, and my dog asleep by the side of the bed. My mitt and bat were in the corner, and second- and third-place trophies cluttered my dresser top.

When I finally did open my eyes, nothing had changed.

I was still in the hospital.

The digital clock read 12:12 a.m. A soft light filtered into the room from the window. Probably the moon. I used the remote to lift the head of my bed.

My mother was asleep in the reclining chair in the corner of the room by the window. She had told me she'd been sleeping there every night. She'd been using the blanket and pillow a nurse had given her on the first night.

The blanket was snuggled close under her chin. Looking at her made me feel hotter. I kicked the blankets and sheets off my legs.

The get-well balloons quivered and swayed, dancing on the ends of their strings, so I knew the air conditioner was on, for all the good it did.

I was surprised I'd fallen asleep at all. Not only was it a hot and sticky night, but besides that, I was going home in the morning. I'd already been in the hospital for twelve days.

I crossed my arms and pushed my head hard into the pillow. I turned it, looking for the cool side. Although I really wanted to get out of the hospital, I couldn't see how things were going to be any better at home. What the heck was the rest of summer going to be like? Where would I be going with a cane? Not to play any baseball games, that's for sure. How would I ever ride my bike, or run around, or do anything fun ever again?

My bike. I loved that thing. I pictured it leaning on its kickstand in our garage. How would I ride if I needed a cane just for normal walking?

Summer never lasts forever. What would I do when school started?

I'd be entering junior high, a new school. I wouldn't be able to hear the teachers. They'd be talking and talking, and even if they talked loudly, I still wouldn't know what they were saying, or what the kids around me were saying.

Or what my friends were saying—if I still had any friends.

Sure, all those fruit baskets and stuff were from my friends, but not really. They were from their parents. Aside from Patrick, did anyone else actually care? I didn't want to be some freak at school, using a cane and forcing everyone to write down everything they needed to say.

Were they all scared of me now? Would anyone want to risk getting close to me? Did they all think they'd get sick, too?

I bit my lip. If it had been Patrick who got sick, would I still want to hang out with him?

Of course I would. Definitely, I would—unless he was still contagious. Then I might wait. Once he wasn't contagious anymore—like I was now—I'd be the first one at the hospital waiting to see him. Especially now, knowing that seeing only your family gets boring real fast.

Well, if no one wanted to be my friend anymore, then maybe I didn't need friends anymore. I was tougher than that, right? I might be deaf, and I might need a cane, but so what? So what?

I didn't really believe what I was telling myself.

On the moveable tray by the bed were the papers from Dr. Allen. I closed my eyes. At first I hadn't wanted to look at them. They were from some article printed off the Internet about the ear. When I finally did read them, they were hard to understand—all technical language. But I got the important part.

I guess losing those hair things ruined my balance. That's why I needed the cane. Dr. Allen had written that he didn't know how long I'd need the cane for—that I had something called "vertigo."

It seems I was weak from being sick, deaf from getting sick, and needed a cane because I was sick. That was some bad bug.

❧

Dad got the day off of work in order to bring me home from the hospital. I was glad to see him when he walked into the room.

"Where's Mom?" Dad wrote on the pad by the bed: *Home, getting ready for you.*

What did *that* mean? I didn't want everyone to make some big deal over me just because I was deaf.

He gathered up the fruit baskets, cookie-grams, flowers, and balloons and took them down to the parking lot to load into the car. I knew someone would eat the fruit. I wanted the cookies. Once my stomach started feeling more normal I planned to shovel them into my mouth. I knew if I ate them now, I wouldn't enjoy them.

I used the cane to get up out of bed, then went around my hospital room taking down the get-well cards Mom had taped to the walls. Although I didn't want to use it, the cane was coming in handy now, helping me balance while I peeled tape off the walls. I was looking at a card Marie had made for me of Whitney when my father came back into the room. I felt ashamed to have been caught leaning on the cane for support.

"I don't need this."

Dad nodded and seemed to try to smile, but finally just looked away instead. Then he pointed to all the cards piled on the bed, and wrote on the pad. *Good friends.*

I shrugged. I wasn't too sure about that.

Soon as you dress we can head home. Need help?

I scoffed, totally annoyed, "I'm deaf, Dad. Not an invalid."

Parents just never do or say the right thing.

CHAPTER 8

When Dad pulled into the driveway, I stepped out of the car and leaned on my cane for support. Maybe I was beginning to understand a few things. The house, the yard, all looked the same. A finch flew by. It flapped its little wings, soared, and landed on the mailbox at the edge of the driveway. Four kids rode by on bicycles. I couldn't hear the bird chirping, or the kids talking as they passed the house. These were sounds—normal, everyday sounds—that I never paid any attention to before.

I slammed the car door. Nothing.

A "Welcome Home, Marco" banner hung over the front door that opened to let out Mom and Marie, and, pushing her way to the front of the line, Whitney. She launched toward me. Her tail wagged back and forth so hard she could hardly run straight. Her jaw moved, but I could not hear the barking.

I lowered to my knees. For a seventy-pound lab, she thought of herself as a small lap dog. She jumped onto my legs and licked my face. I scratched behind her ears. Her hind leg shook; she enjoyed the scratching. I patted her belly and rubbed the top of her head. Then she went back to licking my face.

"Whitney, I missed you, girl. I missed you."

Marie sat down beside us. Whitney licked Marie. She closed her eyes, wrinkled her nose, but did not move away. I watched my sister pet my dog. She saw me looking at her. She stopped petting Whitney. Then, like some kind of animal on the prowl, Marie pounced. Before I knew what was happening, she had wrapped her arms around my neck. She was hugging me so tightly, I could barely breathe.

I hugged her back and, within a split second, the hug was over.

Whitney was up, tongue dangling, tail wagging, and ready for more attention.

A car pulled in the driveway as I got slowly to my feet. I hated the cane, but without it I wasn't sure I'd be able to get up. I felt so tired. If I closed my eyes, I'd fall asleep—right here, outside my house.

I recognized the car. Patrick got out of the back seat. He gave me a big smile, a wave, and then ran over. We shook hands. *Clap, clap, clap*—then the over-the-top, upside-down clap.

Mom and Dad stood close together, arms around each other. Patrick's parents, whom I had never seen together before, got out of the car. His mother held a big cake box.

As we went into the house, I fought back tears. This was supposed to be a party. Everyone around me was smiling, talking, and having a good time. In addition to feeling exhausted and off balance, I wore myself out straining to hear. I concentrated and concentrated on hearing. Nothing happened. I heard nothing at all.

As I wandered through the house, I noticed pens and pads of paper strewn all over the place. Patrick followed me around as I reacquainted myself with the house. He was reminding me of my dog.

I passed on the cake. Patrick brought his piece into the living room and sat with me when I had finally settled in. I was on the recliner by the television set. He sat on the sofa, picked up the remote, and switched it on. What good was the TV to me? Marie and I used to argue about what we'd watch. Rarely did we agree on a show. Now it wouldn't matter; unless a show had subtitle options, watching TV would be pointless.

He must have sensed this because he shut it off.

I thought about closed captioning, where the words people say show up on the TV screen. That would be great for a person who liked reading. I hated reading.

Now that I was deaf, would my loathing for reading have to change? How much more change could I handle? I had to close my eyes.

Someone was shaking me. I guess I'd fallen asleep. Patrick was gone. The clock on the mantel showed it was close to four o'clock. *Wow, I slept for three hours.* I felt like I could close my eyes and sleep three more, but Mom was handing me a pad of paper. I rubbed the sleep out of my eyes and read what she wrote. *Are you hungry?*

"Not really. I want to go up to my room."

Still tired?

Dr. Allen had warned me I'd feel worn out, possibly for weeks. That was certainly how I felt now, but maybe I should try to stay awake. "I am, but I want to go online or something."

Mom helped me up out of the chair and over my sleeping dog. Out front, I saw my dad watching Marie do cartwheels on the lawn. He was clapping for the performance.

Using the cane, I made my way toward the stairs. Whitney, no longer asleep, followed alongside. Impatient with me taking one step at a time upstairs, Whitney charged. When she reached the top step, she turned and stared at me, tongue hanging.

The middle stair always creaked and moaned under my weight. When I'd sneak around—if Marie and I were playing hide-and-seek, or if I didn't want Mom or Dad to know where I was—I skipped over it so the squeaking noise wouldn't give me away. I stepped on the stair now, hard, wishing I could hear it, but I heard nothing. Just the low hum of static I'd been hearing on and off for days.

I finished climbing the stairs with my head hung low.

In my room, Whitney climbed right up onto my bed and lay down at the foot. I stood in the doorway, looking around. Maybe I expected it to be different somehow, now that *I* was different. I can't say what I expected to have changed.

Everything looked the same.

My computer, iPod, posters, and the trophies on the dresser… they were all where I remembered them being.

I picked up the iPod and thumbed it on, then scrolled through pages of downloads. I selected one and let it play; I assumed the music was coming out of the docking station speakers.

I knew what the song was. I knew how the music was supposed to sound— and every intonation of every word.

Staring at the timer did nothing. I heard no music. I heard no words.

I could only watch the blue bars on the digital display rise and fall in time with the unheard beat. Frustrated, I shut the iPod off. I had no use for this. Not anymore.

6∞9

I sat at the desk where I usually did my homework, and switched on the computer. At the search engine prompt, I typed in "Meningitis."

Links to over 234,000,000 sites were available. Hundreds of millions of sites! That seemed like an awful lot of websites for a disease I didn't even know existed until a week ago.

I looked around the room and realized something. Working on the computer was kind of cool. It seemed as good as watching television, or better. Better because I didn't need sound to enjoy the Web. I was sucked into the computer and felt normal being there. I almost laughed—I didn't want to watch closed caption on television because of all the reading... but what was I doing online? Reading.

Maybe closed caption wouldn't be that terrible.

The clock on the monitor showed I'd been online for nearly two hours. I logged off the Internet, hooked the video game unit up to my computer, and popped in that new video game—the one Patrick and I played before I got sick. After two innings, it no longer held my interest. I couldn't hear the crowds cheering or the bat hitting the ball. I couldn't hear the runners grunt as they slid into second. The graphics were still awesome, but without the sound effects, it wasn't the same. It looked like people just going through the motions, kind of like I was.

I noticed that Dad was poking his head into my room. He waved and held up his pad of paper. *How's it going?*

"Come on in, Dad." I switched the screen off and climbed onto the bed. People might think I was lucky that I was still alive and only deaf. It sure didn't feel that way.

Want to play catch?

"No. I'm too tired. Tomorrow, maybe."

He nodded. He started to write something else on the pad.

"I just want to rest," I said, quickly, before he could offer something else for us to do together.

CHAPTER 9

Monday evening, we piled into the car and headed for Batavia High School. They taught American Sign Language there. The introductory course was a night class, and would take place once a week for eight weeks. Marie and I sat at the back of the car. I kept my notebook and pen close by. My cane rested between us.

I kept looking at my hands, studying my fingers. I curled them in and out, making a variety of shapes with them, as if I were already signing. How in the world was I going to learn to communicate with my hands? I got the feeling I'd be walking around with pen and paper for the rest of my life.

I watched Marie talking to Mom and Dad and then saw my father reach for the radio knob. Normally, this would be a time when Marie and I would argue, "I want this song," or "You got to pick the last two songs—it's my turn now!"

I guess—from now on—if Marie wanted a particular station, she'd get no arguments from me. I was forced to listen to static. It hissed inside my brain and was getting a lot worse. I wished I had a remote so I could change channels or just switch off the noise altogether. Closing my eyes, no matter how tightly, didn't make it go away.

Rolling my head from side to side was also useless, but ignoring the static seemed impossible. I looked out the window. Though it was nearly seven at night, the sun was sitting brightly in the sky. It wouldn't get dark until around nine.

I liked Batavia. The way the brick buildings along Main Street were all connected to each other, the small-town store fronts, and even the black streetlight poles dotting the road always cheered me. People were out walking, either carrying shopping bags, ice cream cones, or kids. Some people pushed a stroller, or held onto a dog's leash. There was a lot going on; for a small town, we always seemed to be busy. I spent summers on my bike cruising these streets, knew every inch of the town. Patrick and I would leave our bikes resting against McGill's Diner. Best burgers and sundaes around. The fact that it slammed up against the bowling alley only made Saturdays all the better. Nothing beat bowling a few games, and a big lunch after! The Silver Screen only had two theaters. We didn't get movies as fast as the rest of the world, but when something good was showing, we'd always be first in line for the matinee. Batavia might seem like Hicksville to most people passing through. For me, it was home.

Finally, we pulled into the parking lot. The huge two-story building looked more like a prison than a school. As we walked from the car toward the front doors, I could imagine armed guards on the roof, watching us from behind a coiled roll of barbed wire. I walked slowly and carefully alongside my parents, trying as hard as I could not to use the cane. We walked into the school. Marie ran ahead, turned, and came back. When she noticed I wasn't using the cane, she walked beside me, watching my feet. She looked at me, giving me a thumbs-up sign. I looked down at my own feet and focused.

Inside the school, I searched for something that would let us know we were in the right place. Dad tapped my shoulder and flicked his chin toward a paper sign taped to the wall. The black arrow on the sign directed us down a hallway. Printed below the arrow were three simple letters: *ASL*. He gave me a thumbs-up sign. I tried to smile but I probably just ended up shrugging and looking away. How was this going to work, talking with my hands?

We had all memorized the American Sign Language alphabet. We worked at home on using this alphabet to spell words to each other—fingerspelling— but it was such a slow way of sharing. Dr. Allen had suggested we learn ASL as a family. This would be a better way for us to communicate.

Another sign was taped to a door. Mom opened the door tentatively and stuck her head inside the classroom. Then she turned and nodded at us.

We all followed her in. Maybe seven other people were already in the room, besides the instructor. She was a tall, thin, energetic woman. She shook hands with each of us and pointed at her name, Mrs. Smiley, printed in chalk on the blackboard.

I watched Mom's lips move. Mrs. Smiley closed her eyes and shook her head quickly—"no." She turned around and walked over to the blackboard where she picked up a piece of chalk.

Mom's eyebrows wrinkled on her forehead. She looked at Dad, puzzled.

Mrs. Smiley wrote two words on the board: *I'm Deaf.* She pointed to the word "I'm" and then at her chest. Then she tapped on the word "deaf" before pointing at her lips and then at her ear. *Well, whaddya know?* I couldn't believe it. The teacher was deaf… like me.

She wrote *hearing* on the blackboard. She gestured toward it, and then at her mouth. Twice she ran the tip of her finger up from her bottom lip to her top lip.

Mrs. Smiley led my sister toward the blackboard and showed her the word *deaf*, then the word *hearing*. She held up both thumbs and moved her hands up and down as if her fists were on opposite ends of a teeter-totter. She wrote: *Which one?* She repeated the sign with her thumbs again.

Marie mimicked the sign for hearing by pointing at her lips, and then brushing her fingertip up her lips two times. Mrs. Smiley patted her on the head and handed Marie an *American Sign Language* textbook.

My parents also indicated that they were hearing people, repeating the sign we'd just learned. Mrs. Smiley gave books to them, too, and they sat on either side of Marie in the third row, behind some other students.

For my turn, when she made the teeter-totter sign to ask me which one I was, deaf or hearing, I paused—trying to recall the sign for deaf. What was wrong with me? She'd just taught it to us a few seconds ago. I pointed at my lips and then at my ear.

No. Not right. I shook my head. I pointed at my ear and then at my lips.

She nodded her head, eyes sparkling. The smile she gave me looked different from the one she offered my family. We had something in common.

Mrs. Smiley pointed from her lips to her ear, before nodding that that was correct. Next, she moved her finger from her ear to her lips, and shrugged, nodding, indicating that that was okay, too. She made a fist with her thumb and pinkie sticking out. She moved her hand back and forth, directing the thumb toward her chest. She wrote: *Same thing*. She made the sign again.

I did the sign, *same thing*. Then I signed *deaf* both ways and repeated the sign, *same thing*. She gave me a book and I went over and sat by my dad.

Then Mrs. Smiley wrote one more thing on the board: *Absolutely no talking in class.*

⌒⋙⋘⌒

When we arrived home, I sat at the kitchen table with my parents and I wrote on my pad: *OK. ASL is waaaaaay different than spelling, LOL.*

To make words in ASL, I had to put my hands and fingers into certain positions and then move them and my arms in specific ways to form words.

Some of the signs readily made sense—like *Hello* in ASL; it's a salute. Even hearing people say "Hello" like that all the time.

Dad wrote: *One thing I learned, ASL is not just about learning to speak with hands. Everything goes into making a sentence complete. The whole body needs to be used.*

Mom nodded in agreement. She added: *Use your body for punctuation. Raise your eyebrows to ask a question. Or, make a mad face for an exclamation point.*

The teacher had showed us how effective combining signs with actions could be. She taught us how to sign, excuse me. First she held out one hand, palm up. Then she brushed the fingertips of the other hands down the palm, over and over. When she did this she stood as stiff as a board in front of class and brought her hands up to her chest. She repeated the sign for *excuse me* and kept her eyes focused straight ahead, and her jaw tight.

Though she had done the sign correctly, she had written on the board: *Does not look sincere.*

Next she showed us the better way to sign *excuse me*. She stood bent slightly forward, raised her shoulders, and made a gentle, kind of questioning face. She signed, *excuse me*, and this time, it looked like she meant it.

I took the pad and wrote: *Toughest thing, learning to use my hands to make words, or body to punctuate. No! Hardest thing—understanding the order of words. Even though ASL is Eng. words, the sentences don't sound normal.*

Mom and Dad nodded. Dad rolled his eyes. Mom sighed.

A person wouldn't sign, *Hey, did you see that great baseball game on television last night?* Instead, the words are all over the place. With signing, I had to use my eyes and move my body to make a point. So I'd have to open my eyes wide, and sign, *Baseball game last night see you, finish?*

If we keep practicing, it will eventually get easier, Dad wrote.

I wasn't so sure. I shrugged, picked up my book and tucked it under my arm.

Where are you going? Mom wrote.

I hooked my cane over my forearm. With one hand, I made a fist. With the other, I made like a gun, with my thumb up and first finger pointing out. Then I pretended to scrub the fist back and forth over that extended finger. *To practice.*

I headed for my room.

CHAPTER 10

I wanted to hide from it all. I did my best to stay in my room for as long as I could. Here I was, home for nearly a week, and I still felt exhausted all the time. Hobbling around on a cane made me feel uncomfortable. I knew everyone was staring at me. Like being deaf wasn't bad enough?

I spent most of the time on my bed, either studying my ASL book, or, more often than not, staring at the closed bedroom door.

Sometimes, if I saw the doorknob start to turn, I'd close my eyes and pretend to be asleep. No one ever tried to wake me if I was sleeping. It seemed like the only thing I could to do in order to hide from everyone and not worry them. Sometimes I kept them closed so long I'd actually fall asleep—I guess because I didn't want to risk opening them and see anyone standing over me. And since I was deaf, I couldn't hear a person leave the room, or shut the door like I could when I used to fake being asleep before… before… losing my hearing.

This morning, however, I didn't feel like staying in my room. I picked up my mitt and a ball and went into the kitchen. Dad sat at the table drinking coffee and reading the Sunday paper.

"Dad," I said, to get his attention.

He looked up.

I showed him my mitt. His eyes lit up and his mouth spread into a huge smile. He held up a finger, asking me to wait—or stay right where I was—and hurried out of the kitchen. A few seconds later he returned with his mitt and his Yankees cap on his head.

I tried not to lean on the cane too much as we went out into the yard. I was working real hard at walking without it. We stood maybe twenty-five, thirty feet away from each other. I dropped the cane to the ground. We started slowly. I threw the ball to Dad. It felt awkward, like I might lose my balance.

But I didn't. And I also didn't hear the sound of the ball slap into his mitt. It was all very clumsy. It had been weeks since Dad and I played catch. We used to practice pitches every night when he got home from work, or before a game.

He looked happy. I wasn't sure how I felt. It was cool being outside throwing the ball around. But it was so different. I wanted so badly to hear the ball cut through the air and slam into the mitt. I looked at my glove, like something might be wrong with it, instead of wrong with me. Like it was made with defective leather or something.

After a while, when he threw the ball to me, then crouched into a catcher's position, I knew what he wanted. We were done warming up. He wanted to see if I could fire one into his glove.

I swallowed hard and took a deep breath. I stood sideways, arms down, hands in front of me. My right hand was in my glove, cradling the ball. I took another deep breath and wound up. I lifted my arms and brought up my leg, kicked my leg up high—toward my chest.

The inside of my head became fuzzy, my vision blurred. Then I felt my left knee buckle and I fell backwards onto the ground. I guess I knocked the wind out of myself, because I lay there gasping, unable to breathe. The ball rolled out of my hand. I wasn't really hurt, but I covered my face with my mitt when I saw my dad running toward me. I could see him through the finger cracks in the mitt. "I'm okay," I said. "Leave me alone. I'm okay!"

Dad held up his left hand, palm facing me. He brought up his right hand and touched the fingertips into the palm of his left hand. *Again?*

I shook my head. "I want to go in."

Dad signed: *Again*. Then he placed the palm of his right hand over his heart and moved it around in circles against his chest. *Please.*

I looked up at the sky, a few puffy white clouds hung against a clear, sunny blue. I closed my eyes. I guess I wasn't ready to go back inside. "Sure," I said.

He handed me the ball and took position where he was catching. I saw the corner of his mouth curl up into a half-smile. This time when I wound up, I concentrated on my left knee, on not toppling over. I pitched a fastball but it went wild. Dad jumped up and stretched, reaching for the ball. It soared over his head and into the bushes along the chainlink fence.

My legs wobbled and wiggled, but I managed to stay on my feet. Just tossing the ball around, I could do. Pitching would take some work. Like learning sign language.

CHAPTER 11

MID-JULY

I t seemed like I had just entered a chat room for deaf people on the computer when I felt a gentle tap on the shoulder. I jumped and spun around. Mom stood with a sort of apologetic expression on her face and held a fist against her chest, rubbing it around in small circles over her heart. *Sorry.*

My family usually got my attention by switching lights on and off or gently tapping me on the shoulder. When I could hear, I might be in my room listening to music with headphones on, eyes closed, and Marie would sneak up behind me and grab my shoulders. I'd scream loud enough to rattle the windows. The tapping thing wasn't easy to get used to.

I didn't scream this time, but I could have—until I saw the pad Mom carried. It had an important word written on it in capital letters: *LUNCH.*

Taking sign languages classes a night a week helped us communicate better—but we were only two weeks into the lessons. We had learned lots of important words like *look, class, please, sorry, yes, no, why, how, feel, tired, warm, thirsty, scared, nice, meet, practice, study, help*... but we needed to learn so many more in order to use signing all the time instead of writing everything on a pad of paper.

"Got it," I said. "I'll be right there."

I turned back to the computer. *Got to go*, I typed. *Time for lunch.*

Most people in the chat room typed out sentences as if they were signing in ASL. One chatter replied: *Eat lunch, come back when done finish you?* I knew what he meant in regular English: *When you finish eating lunch, will you come back online?*

Whitney, who'd been asleep at my feet, got up and followed me down to the kitchen. At my place at the table, Mom had set a plate of reheated pasta in front of me. Capolini. A thin noodle, and my favorite. I sat and Whitney laid back down, resting her chin on top of my feet and falling easily back to sleep. I twirled pasta onto my fork, shoved it into my mouth and slurped up a straggling string, sauce splashing my nose.

"This one kid in the chat room—he was hard of hearing first, then became completely deaf—well, he can read lips and only signs some of the time."

Mom sat next to me. She wrote: *How old was he when he became deaf?*

"Fifty-four." I shrugged.

She raised her eyebrows. *54 is not a kid!* I shrugged again. "I'm trying to learn lip-reading, but it isn't as easy you might think. Go ahead, say something."

Mom's lips moved. I rolled my eyes. "You said, 'I love you.' That's too easy. Say something hard."

Mom shook her head. *You're wrong. I didn't say "I love you." I said, "Elephant shoes."*

I laughed. "You got me. Okay, try another one."

Mom looked up, over my head. I turned to look myself, but nothing was there. Then she was walking past me and out of the kitchen. Whitney was up, her lips pulled back into a snarl. Though I could not hear her, I knew she'd begun barking.

"Ma? Mom, what is it?"

I got up and left the kitchen, and ran into the living room to see what was going on. Mom was at the front door, talking to someone.

Marie stood beside her. "Marie," I said, "Is everything okay? What's going on?"

She shrugged, putting the tips of her fingers from her right hand to her forehead, and then—almost like in a salute—she pulled them away. *I don't know.*

Mom let a man into the house. He wore blue pants and a blue shirt. The tool belt strapped around his waist hung low on one hip. Holstered in a leather pouch was a cordless power drill. He looked like some mechanical gunslinger, a robot with a power drill instead of a six-shooter, but I figured he was just a repairman.

Whitney was still not comfortable with all of this.

I held her back by the collar. Marie helped.

Marie was the one who seemed to catch on to ASL the easiest. I worked at it each night, the way I used to work at pitching with Dad. I also practiced in front of a mirror. Not Marie. She paid attention in class and, for some reason, the signs just stuck with her. I liked watching her sign—it was easy to figure out what she was saying.

He waved to Marie and me as Mom led him down to the basement.

"Who's that?" I signed the question, *Who he?*

Marie picked up a pad from off the coffee table. *Dryer broke.*

"I was talking to Mom and then she ran out of the kitchen. I didn't know what was going on. I wasn't too worried or anything until Whitney got up and looked upset."

The doorbell, she wrote.

The doorbell. I knew that much now. This wasn't the first time something like this had happened. The phone would ring, or someone would be at the door and I wouldn't have a clue what was going on.

Dad, Mom and I sat at the kitchen table. Marie poured dog food from a bag into Whitney's bowl and then joined us. Two catalogues were open on the table. Together, we added items to a growing list on a sheet of paper. The house needed new things now that I was deaf. Many of the items we'd already ordered; they either hadn't come in yet, or we were waiting for someone to come and do the installation.

Mom got all excited and pointed at an item. It was a vibrator we could put under my mattress. It would hook up to my alarm clock and shake me awake in the mornings. She nodded her head in jerky motions. *Fine,* she signed, tapping her thumb in the center of her chest. The sign had more than one meaning. The way she was doing it now also meant "awesome." We added it to the list.

Dad wrote, *Any word on when the electrician will be here to wire the lights to the phone and doorbell?*

Sometime next week—that's also when the TTY machine should be here, Mom wrote. The text telephone, or TTY, was really no different than texting on a cell phone. Just this one was plugged into the wall.

Dad smiled at me. It felt like we were looking through a toy catalogue at Christmastime. I guess that's why I wondered if he was worried about money. "The alarm clock for the bed can wait, Dad," I said. "It's summer. And Whitney usually licks my face to let me know she needs to go outside. Besides, it's not like I have to get up early for school."

School. I didn't like thinking about that. I put a hand on my stomach.

Mom pointed at me and then ran her middle finger up the center of her chest twice. She fingerspelled *OK. You feel okay?*

I made a fist, like the letter "A" in sign language—with my thumb against the side of my finger, not lying across the front of the first few—and made as if I were knocking on a door. *Yes.* Then I signed, *Tired.*

Go rest. We'll look at this stuff later, wrote Mom.

CHAPTER 12

The next day, I sat on the living room sofa and looked through my ASL textbook. Out the window, I saw Patrick ride up the driveway on his bike. He climbed off, removed his helmet, and hooked the straps over the handlebars. I hadn't seen him since the day I came home from the hospital. I grabbed my cane and hurried out of the living room toward the stairs.

Mom, coming down the stairs with the laundry basket, held out her hand, thumb up, pinkie down, as if we were about to shake hands. She ran the first finger of her other hand down the open palm. *What?*

"I'm going up to my room to lie down," I said. "I'm really tired."

I ran into my room, jumped on the bed, and closed my eyes. I knew that if she peeked in, she'd think I was resting or had even fallen asleep and would leave me alone.

I didn't have all my strength back, or my balance, or my hearing. However, in the few more times I'd practiced playing ball with my dad, my legs hadn't danced around and made me fall. I carried the cane around everywhere, but didn't actually need to use it as much. Little by little, I worked on walking without it. If I took my time, I walked fine.

I waited a long time and then opened my eyes.

Patrick sat at my desk. He stared at me and held up a pad of paper. In big blue marker letters he'd written: *Worst. Fake-sleeping. Ever.*

"Is not." I sat up. The sun streaming in the window did not affect Patrick. He wore his Yankees ball cap tipped low so the bill shaded his eyes from the light. He drummed his fingertips on the desk. I imagined the sound of the *tap-tap-tap-tap*, as I watched his knuckles move in a rolling wave.

I didn't know what to say or what to do. He almost felt like a stranger.

Patrick wrote something else on the pad. *It's weird you can talk, but can't hear.*

I shrugged. It didn't feel weird to me. It just annoyed me, like being able to eat but not taste food. What was weird was the static that came and went. Each time the hissing filled an ear I felt my heart skip a beat. Because each time I thought I'd get better and have my hearing restored.

He wrote: *Makes me forget you're…*

I looked at the three periods at the end of what Patrick had written and sighed. I didn't want to have this conversation. I gave the writing tablet back to my friend. "That what? That I'm deaf?"

Patrick nodded. *I forget sometimes, too,* I wanted to tell him. Instead, I kept silent.

"I'm really still kind of tired." I stood up, and without the cane, walked toward the window. The funny thing was, I was really glad to see him. But I also felt sort of mad at him. Why did he have to be so persistent? He couldn't possibly know what my life was like now. Why would he even want to? How could he know how much concentration it took for me to walk without my cane? He could walk just fine. He could hear just fine. "I'm going to lie back down and try to get some sleep or something."

Patrick picked up the marker and wrote something else and handed the tablet over. I read what he wrote.

"Oh? My mother told you I was reading?"

He took back the pad and wrote some more, then handed it to me. "Yeah," I said. "My dad and I go out and play catch."

He took the pad back and wrote again.

I read what he had written out loud. "Big ball game at the park. Don't waste summer here. Let's enjoy our… vaccation!" A baseball game. I had practiced throwing with dad, but not hitting. I didn't even know if I could swing a bat. Or, if I could, whether I would be able to stay on my feet. I pointed at the last word. "You spelled 'vacation' wrong. There's only one 'c.'"

Patrick slapped the tablet out of my hand. He picked my mitt up off my trophy shelf. He tossed the mitt at me and walked out of the bedroom, waving for me to follow.

I watched Patrick stop at the stairs. He turned to look at me. For at least a minute we stared at each other. He kept waving for me to follow him. I kept shaking my head, *no*—a battle of wills. He put his hands together, begging. I rolled my eyes. Finally, I nodded my head and sighed. I plucked my baseball cap from off the bedpost, slipped it on over my head, tucked my mitt under my arm and stared for a moment at the cane. I decided not to bring it. I closed the door behind me as I followed after my friend, who smiled victoriously as he started down the stairs.

Mom was sitting on the sofa in the living room. She had a basket of clean clothes at her feet, with neatly folded piles on the sofa all around her. She signed, *Where are you going?*

I made two fists, one on top of the other, like I was gripping a baseball bat. *Baseball.*

She made the kind of face she always made when I told her I felt sick and thought I should stay home from school. She even moved toward me like she might reach out and touch my forehead to see if I had a fever. But she just touched the fingertip of her first finger to her chin and arced it forward. *You sure?*

"Yeah, I'm sure." I pretended to knock on a door with my fist, the sign for *Yes.* You think she'd finally be happy I was going to do something other than mope around.

Okay, she signed.

Patrick followed me into the kitchen. I filled two water bottles with ice. At the sink, I let the water run until it was nice and cold. Looking out the window, I saw Whitney running through the yard with a tennis ball in her mouth. I strained to see where she was running. Marie squatted low. Whitney ran up to her, dropped the ball and paced in circles. Marie stood up, threw the ball toward the end of the yard then wiped the slobber from the ball onto her jeans.

Patrick and I went into the garage. I pushed up the kickstand on my bike. I took a deep breath. What would riding a bike be like? Was I crazy trying to ride for the first time in front of a friend?

It should be easy, I told myself as I strapped on my helmet. But I wasn't sure I believed it. What if Patrick wanted to ride really fast? "I haven't ridden my bike since, you know, since getting home from the hospital."

Patrick smiled and nodded. He gave me a thumbs-up sign and pedaled out of the driveway, slowly. He understood. I sat on the bike, keeping both feet planted on the cement floor in the garage. I put a foot on a pedal, balancing on one leg. So far, so good.

Patrick stopped, turned, and waved me on.

I leaned forward and tried pedaling. The bike wobbled and the handlebars jerked left and right. The pedals seemed to force my feet off them. I stood and straddled the center bar. Up ahead, Patrick had stopped and was watching me. He didn't look impatient. Instead, he stared at me with a worried expression on his face. It made me feel like I was a baby about to take his first step.

I told myself I wasn't going to fall.

I tried again. Once I managed to pedal and the bike started moving, balancing on two wheels became easier. I was afraid to do anything but stay seated as I pedaled. I used to love to stand and pedal—especially when I wanted to go faster. Right now, however fast I was going was fast enough.

Patrick nodded and smiled, and started toward the park.

Normally, nothing could beat the feeling of freedom I got when my bike was cruising down a street so fast that pedaling became pointless. This afternoon, however, I had to pedal slowly, falling farther and farther behind Patrick. My feet kept sliding off the pedals. The bike insisted on wobbling. I didn't want to fall. What used to be so easy, now suddenly felt impossible.

A car pulled out in front of me. I skidded to a stop by the curb. The driver, with his window down, looked like he was yelling at me. He made a fist and shook it.

"I'm deaf," I yelled. "I can't hear you."

The guy arched an eyebrow and curled his lips, like *yeah, right, kid.* He took off and a plume of exhaust shot out of the car's tailpipe. It made me close my eyes and cough. I realized that I'd almost been run over. The driver had probably honked his horn and figured I'd get out of the way.

My face burning, I thought about going home—I wanted to go home and forget all about this—but then I looked both ways and made sure no traffic was coming and forced myself to start again.

I needed to depend on my eyes twice as much now. I wouldn't hear the honk of an oncoming car. This time, I'd been lucky. But what if the driver couldn't stop next time? What if the driver kept honking, assuming I could hear, thinking I'm just some punk kid ignoring the warning?

Who would have thought I could ever miss the sound of traffic. The silence felt ghoulish, and I broke out into a sweat—a sweat that had nothing to do with the July heat.

I pedaled past the diner, bowling alley, and movie theater. I guessed going for burgers and sundaes wasn't out of the question. But movies? Would Patrick and I still catch matinees together? What about bowling... I could barely ride my bike. I couldn't imagine running down the approach with a sixteen-pound ball in my hand. Didn't *want* to imagine it.

When I reached the park and got off my bike, I looked back at the road I'd just traveled down. Cars, trucks—buses—driving everywhere. I had to be crazy being deaf and riding my bike to the park.

Forget it. I'd made it this far. That's what counted. At least that was what I tried to tell myself. I knew it was going to take a few more moments before I could start breathing normally again.

⹂

At the bike rack, I locked my bike alongside Patrick's and groaned. Patrick looked at me with a questioning expression, scrunching his brow and holding his hands palms up, in an *are-you-okay* way.

"My notebook and pen," I said, trying to speak softly. I didn't want to attract attention in case I talked too loudly. "I left them at home."

Patrick said something. I shrugged and leaned closer—as if this might help me hear what he said! But I couldn't help it. It was a natural reflex. Patrick placed a hand on my shoulder and repeated his question, obviously speaking more slowly, perhaps even more loudly. His lips moved in an exaggerated slow motion. I still had no idea what he was saying. "I'm not a lip-reader," I explained.

Patrick used his finger and in the soft dirt wrote: *Need them?*

I looked hard at my friend—didn't he get it? "Look at what we just went through. The notebook and pen would keep everyone from stooping over and writing in the dirt. I don't want to go out there and look even more stupid. I already feel like an idiot."

Patrick wrote: *Friends,* and underlined it.

In other words, don't feel stupid. We're all friends here. Yeah. Well, then why did I feel so out of place?

I fixed my ball cap so that the hair along my forehead was tucked up inside. I desperately wanted to fit in, to feel normal again. I looked at the ball field. I recognized the kids throwing a ball around, getting under pop flies, and taking practice swings on deck. The truth was I missed everyone—and playing the game.

Today would be different than playing catch with Dad. We were going to choose up sides and have a game, a real sandlot game. I slid my fingers into my mitt and punched my other hand into the palm of the glove. It felt natural.

Patrick touched me on the shoulder and motioned for me to follow. I did, but became uneasy. Suddenly, a part of me longed to go home. My emotions were jumping all over the place. These might be my friends, but I was a different person now. And they were different, too, in a way. They were different because I couldn't hear them.

CHAPTER 13

P atrick and I walked out onto the field. The kids stopped what they were doing to watch us. I knew most of them, either from school or from Little League. Jordan was there and some of the kids from his team who went to a different school than I did, and some other kids I didn't know at all.

Tyrone ran right over and clapped me on the back, which broke the ice. Everyone else came over, too, like some fast-moving herd of buffalo or something. In an instant, I was surrounded. Kids waved, slapped me on the head and on the back as a way of saying hello. It almost hurt smiling that much. Actually, I was almost giggling. I realized I had forgotten what that felt like. People's lips moved. They had to be shooting questions at me, like asking about where I'd been and how I was feeling. For the moment, I was thankful that I didn't have my notebook and pen. I might wind up spending the whole time answering written questions. I could see Patrick doing a lot of talking—perhaps explaining as best he could how things have been going for me the last several weeks.

I watched him talk, his hands moving like crazy. What was wrong with me? He'd wanted to see me since I got home from the hospital and what did I do? I made my mother keep him away. Some friend I turned out to be. But *he* didn't give up. He kept calling. And though I ignored the calls, that didn't stop him from coming over. I put a hand on his shoulder while he talked. He flashed me a wink then went right on moving his mouth.

The sun was out, and though I couldn't hear it, I felt the cooling breeze. The sky was blue, and even if I couldn't hear the birds singing, I saw them flying around and perching on tree branches. The baseball diamond's infield and outfield were freshly mown. The smell was so strong it tickled my nostrils, threatening a forced sneeze.

I watched as the captains chose up teams. Jordan got picked fast. So did Patrick. They were on opposite teams. I saw a kid on Jordan's team look at me and whisper something in his ear. When the captain pointed at me, Jordan stopped him and said something. The captain did not choose me.

Patrick's captain eventually picked me. I tried to smile as I joined the other players on my team, but wondered what they had all been talking about.

We were up to bat first.

Patrick pointed at me and then pretended to pitch the ball.

"You want to know if I'm going to be able to pitch?" I asked.

He nodded.

I thought about playing catch with my father that first time after getting home from the hospital. The balance thing was not as big a problem anymore, but it was still an issue. I'd feel like a total loser if I threw a pitch and fell down in front of everyone. "Nah, I'm not pitching. Not today."

He looked a little confused by my answer, but what could he do? We sat side by side on the bench along the first-base line. I could hardly concentrate on the game. Aside from throwing a ball around, Dad and I had yet to practice hitting. When I was up, Patrick handed me a batting helmet. I wished I had thought to try this out with my father. I put the helmet on. Throwing a ball and keeping my balance was one thing. Swinging a bat as hard as I could… that was something else altogether. I placed my hand on my belly and swallowed hard.

Patrick wrote in the dirt: *2 outs*. I scanned the infield: no one on base.

What was I doing here? How long had it been since I'd swung a bat? Only weeks, but it felt like… felt more like forever.

As I walked up to home plate I saw some kids, on both teams, clapping. I felt a small sense of encouragement and hoped it might be for me.

I surprisingly felt good being up to bat. I felt good standing in the box, getting ready for the pitch. But it was also so different. I was acutely aware of the hissing in my ears. I longed to hear chants and taunts like I usually did when I was up at bat. I wanted desperately to hear people calling out my name, or any name, or *anything*, for that matter. As I stood there watching the pitcher, I envisioned cracking one out of the park. I pictured myself running the bases at a slow jog, enjoying a sense of victory.

The pitch came in fast. I swung, spun around, and fell to my knees. I missed it, I guessed. I would have at least liked the usual consolation of hearing the ball smack into the catcher's glove.

Patrick started toward me, but I held up my hand to stop him. I used the bat like a cane and got back up on my feet. While I dusted myself off, I fought back tears. I didn't want to cry out here, not now, not with all of my friends around. *No way.*

I didn't look around. If the guys were laughing, I didn't want to see that.

I dug the toe of my left shoe into the dirt for better footing and concentrated on the pitcher.

Again, the ball came in fast. I swung, but not as hard as I had the first time.

I felt impact as the ball connected with the bat. I took a moment, but only a moment, to watch as the ball sailed toward third base. Then, as my coaches always instructed us, I forgot about the ball and concentrated on running. I ran as best I could toward first base—carefully, making sure I planted each foot on the baseline. I concentrated on not tripping and on keeping my balance and on ignoring the buzzing and hissing inside my head.

Jordan, on first, should have been in position, the toe of his shoe on the edge of the first base bag, ready for someone from left field to throw him the ball. Instead, he was standing with his mitt tucked under his arm, as if he was bored. But as I stepped on first, I saw that Jordan was saying something and moving his hands to shoo me away.

"Foul?" I asked. Jordan nodded. I turned around and headed back toward home. I felt a little foolish. I had hit foul balls before and run all the way to first—that's what happened when you concentrated on running. No big deal. Except now I didn't trust myself. I was too dependent on what others saw and heard.

I went back to home plate and picked up the bat. The static had died away and now I heard nothing at all. It was almost peaceful. For a moment, I closed my eyes.

As I stood in the batter's box, it didn't seem like team against team. It felt more like *me* against *them*, and that frustrated me. I wanted to scream, but I wouldn't be able to hear it, anyway. How satisfying could that be?

I lifted the bat and waited for the next pitch. When it came, I swung as hard as I could. I felt the connection and kept my balance. The ball flew toward third base. I ran as fast as I could toward first. Again, Jordan looked relaxed.

So I stopped running.

Next thing I knew, Jordan was calling me out with his thumb over his shoulder. I nodded, figuring the third baseman had caught the ball.

Then, all of a sudden, Jordan looked ready to catch the ball. He planted his left foot on first base and spread his mitt open wide. I turned in time to see the kid in left field throw the ball to Jordan. Confused, I watched Jordan catch it, take a few steps toward me, reach out and tag me.

I cocked my head to one side, looking at Jordan, my expression asking, "What's up?"

Jordan winked at me and smiled. Though I could not lip-read, I knew he mouthed the word *now*. Then he pointed at my chest and used the out hand signal with his thumb. He didn't need to worry. I got the gist, only too well. *Now, you're out.*

It had been a fair ball, and no one had caught it.

I was about to freak out and let Jordan have it. "What was that? You tricked me? You tricked me, Jordan? Is that funny? You think that's funny?"

Jordan's smug smile vanished. He held up both of his hands, as if surrendering. Again I was able to read his lips. One word: *Joke.*

My hands curled into fists. I raised my arms and shoved Jordan. Without missing a beat, Jordan shoved back.

Patrick emerged and shoved Jordan even harder. Jordan stumbled and fell. Everyone gathered around.

Jordan looked nervously from face to face, his mouth moved. Looked like he was saying, *What? I was just goofing around.*

The other kids didn't look like they thought it was funny.

I remembered a time when Mom and Dad had taken us to a carnival when I'd been much younger, and Marie was still in a stroller. It had been dark out and everything glowed with colorful, flashing lights. People talked and yelled and tripped over the stroller. People on the rides screamed and laughed. The games people played made loud noises. It was too much commotion all at once. Marie had scrunched her eyes up, like she might be trying to block out everything, all the chaos. I remember being afraid and wishing I was in the stroller, too, able to close my eyes and have everything disappear.

I felt that way now with everyone getting involved. Their mouths moved quickly. Kids kicked at the dirt. I had no idea what was being said. Was all of it about me? Did everyone think Jordan had been wrong? Some of the kids—the ones I did not know—looked like they might be on Jordan's side. I closed my eyes regardless, feeling nothing short of humiliated.

Then someone else pushed Patrick.

I backed away from the gang of kids and walked over to the bike rack. I unlocked my bike, got on and rode toward home. I wasn't worried about cars, or losing my balance. I focused on the road ahead of me and pedaled as fast as I dared. I was a little frightened, but not of the traffic.

I hated being deaf.

CHAPTER 14

When I got home, my mother and Marie were unloading the dishwasher. Whitney was asleep under the table. Her ears twitched, and her eyes opened some. But then she went back to sleep.

When Mom saw me, she signed: *How was the game?*

"Fine. I'm going to take a nap." I knew I must sound angry. I couldn't hide my mood. I hurried upstairs and into my room. Before I could turn to close the door, Whitney rushed past me. She sat by the side of my bed. Her tail did not wag, as if she sensed how I was feeling.

I stood in the middle of my room, furious. I should have known it wasn't going to work, trying to play ball with my former friends. I wondered if I'd be able to do anything with them again. I was really on my own now.

I sat on the bed and patted her head, scratching lightly behind the ears. That got her tail wagging. My ASL book was open on the desk and, beside it, the ASL dictionary. I picked up both and moved them to my bed.

Dr. Allen had said that I'd spend the next year in some pretty intense ASL programs. He tried to assure me it would be easier than I expected. I remember wondering how that could be. I only received a "C" grade in English last year, but he was right. So far, because I worked hard at it, learning ASL hadn't been too tough.

In that same conversation, he'd also told my parents and me about some school in Rochester, a school for deaf and hard-of-hearing people.

I hadn't wanted to think about school. Why would I want to go to a school with deaf people?

Then again, why would I want to go to a school that *wasn't* for deaf people? Why did I even have to go to school anymore? What was the point? Dr. Allen had said that if I went to junior high with Patrick, the school would be responsible for getting me an interpreter—someone who would go with me to each class and turn everything the teacher was saying into sign language so I'd know what was being taught. As if that wasn't bad enough, I would also have a person taking notes for me.

I hated that idea. I could just see it. Who would want to be the center of attention like that with an interpreter and a note-taker following them around? And what about when I wasn't in class, like at lunchtime? There was no way some interpreter would want to write down everything that other kids were saying just so I wouldn't be left out of the conversation. How many notebooks would I go through when I sat down to eat with my friends—that is, if I had any friends to sit with? There was no way I'd invite some interpreter to lunch with us just so I could try fitting in. A square peg. A round hole. No way. I was definitely on my own, no doubt about it.

⏳

I looked up from my ASL book and saw Dad outside my door. How long had he been standing there? He waved to me, indicating he'd just got back. He worked Saturdays when he could. I don't think he liked doing it, but he always said that he couldn't turn down an opportunity to make some extra money.

Can I come in? he signed from the doorway.

I shrugged.

What were you doing?

"Practicing signing sentences," I said.

Show me.

I signed a sentence. "That was, 'You lied to me,'" I explained. "Here's another." I signed the sentence. "That one was, 'You give me a pain in the butt.'"

Dad shook his head, as if at a momentary loss for words. He signed again. *What happened?* Mom must have told him I looked upset. He sat next to me on the bed. He picked up a tablet and pen. *Mom says you've been up here a while.*

I nodded. "Studying."

You played ball with Pat and some guys?

After I read what he wrote, I just nodded, looked back down at my book and pretended to be so interested that it was hard to look away from the pages.

He put the tablet on the textbook. *How'd it go?*

I sighed, closed the book and pushed back on the bed. "I hit the ball and was running to first base. Jordan told me I was out, so I stopped running.

Then the guy in left field throws him the ball and Jordan tags me out on the baseline. Dad, he treated me like some kind of idiot. Just because I can't hear doesn't mean I'm stupid."

That's awful, Dad wrote. *But I don't think Jordan thought you were stupid.*

"No? What did he think he was doing, then? Just trying to get a laugh at my expense? He made me feel stupid." I folded my arms across my chest. Even though I didn't want to talk about it, it felt good telling my dad. I had to unfold my arms, and wipe my eyes.

"Mom told me Patrick stopped by and called twice wanting to make sure I was all right. He told her he'd nearly beat up Jordan," I shook my head. "She wasn't too happy to hear that."

Dad clapped a hand on my back, rubbed my shoulder and smiled. *No, she wasn't.*

"I left him, Dad," I said. "Here's Patrick, my best friend, sticking up for me—and I left him. What kind of a friend does that make me? I acted like some coward. He's never going to want to hang out with me again. I can't play ball like I used to and I run at the first sign of trouble."

I grabbed my pillow and buried my face in it. Dad tapped me on the shoulder. He showed me the tablet. *You just told me Pat stopped by and that he called a bunch of times. Why would he do that if you weren't still his friend?*

"So he could tell me we *weren't* friends, that's why."

Dad shook his head. *I don't think so,* he signed.

"Dad, I've been thinking. I want us to go visit that school in Rochester, the one Dr. Allen told us about. I know summer isn't over, but I really don't think I want to go back to my school in the fall. I'm not ready for that—not yet."

Dad just stared at me.

"I don't want to be around people like Jordan," I said. "I don't need that. In school, Dad, there are going to be more people like Jordan than like Patrick."

That's not fair, Dad wrote. *You have to give the kids in school a chance.*

"Why? What chance did Jordan give me?"

It's still July, Dad wrote.

"Let's just go look at it. Please."

The school's in Rochester, Dad wrote, *an hour away. I'm not sure how that can work. You won't see your friends as much if you change schools.*

"What friends?" I huffed.

Patrick, Dad wrote, underlining it for emphasis.

I looked away from the pad. "It won't matter where I go to school. If he wants, we'll still be friends."

True, Dad wrote. *What about other friends?*

"What about them, Dad? Unless they start taking sign language classes like us, what will we have in common? How will we be able to talk to each other? Don't you get it, Dad? I'm deaf. I can't hear anything at all. No one can talk to me without writing things down on paper in that stupid notebook. My life sucks!" I hated the way it felt, talking and talking without hearing a word I said. I imagined my words coming out slurred and mispronounced. There was no way of knowing how I sounded.

Dad put his hands on my shoulders.

I moved a little closer toward him. "I don't know why this had to happen to me. Why me? What did I ever do to deserve this?" I knew I'd raised my voice. I could feel it in my throat, hot like fire.

Dad wrote: *It's not an easy question to answer.*

I stood up. "You have no idea what this is like. You can never know what this feels like." I knocked everything off the top of my dresser with a sweep of my arm. I felt the vibrations through my feet when everything hit the floor. "Did you hear the noise that made, Dad? I didn't. If you make me go back to that other school, do you know how many other things I won't be able to hear? Huh? Try, *everything.* I won't be able to hear anything going on around me. I'll be more than just left out, Dad, I'll be totally alone."

Dad wrote for a few minutes. I didn't feel like hanging around waiting for him to finish. This wasn't his fault, but that didn't matter. I turned the knob on the bedroom door, but Dad put a hand on my shoulder and gave me the tablet.

I never said you couldn't go to a different school. Mom and I want to help you, and support you. You are not a little kid. If you wanted to go back to your old school, then we'd help you adjust. If you want to go visit the school in Rochester, then we'll make an appointment ASAP. OK?

I looked at my father. I didn't think anyone else could understand what I was going through. Though I was hurting inside, I knew that all the things I'd said had caused him pain, too. "I just can't explain what this is like, Dad, the way it feels, the way my life has changed," I said.

Dad looked at me thoughtfully for a moment and then took his time writing: *You're right—I have no idea what you are going through, what it feels like.*

I would trade places with you if I could. You may not believe me, but I would... in a heartbeat. And if you like, I'll stuff plugs in my ears for as long as you want me to, I'll wear them to work if you think that will help me understand what you are going through.

I tried to give him a smile, though I really wanted to cry and hug him. Instead, I pulled open the bedroom door. Before walking out of the room and leaving my father alone, I said, "Thanks, Dad. That means a lot."

He acted out putting in earplugs, then pointed to himself.

I shook my head. "It's not the same thing." It could never be the same thing. "Even if you couldn't hear a sound, you'd always know that if you wanted, you could take the plugs out."

I slammed the door shut—nothing. My point was made: only silence.

Chapter 15

I saw the sign on the Interstate welcoming us to "Rochester, An All-America City." Overall, the trip was supposed to take less than an hour from Batavia, but it seemed to last a lifetime. Just when I wondered if we'd ever make it, Mom turned and signed: *Almost there.*

We'd received all kinds of brochures in the mail two days after Dad called and made the appointment for a visit. At first I flipped through the stuff, thinking, *who cares about the history of a school?* But bits and pieces caught my interest, so I went back and read it all. I thought it was cool that the school was started in the nineteenth century by a married couple with a deaf daughter.

As we first drove up on the school's campus, it looked to me like nothing but a few big old buildings. The property was lined with trees. As my father pulled into the small parking lot, I was surprised by the actual size of the place. The trees no longer blocked my view. I noticed more buildings scattered over the property. A woman led young kids from one building to another. Two teenaged boys threw a football back and forth, and a group of young girls sat on a picnic table under a small maple tree busily talking to each other using sign language.

We'd been told that summer school was in session, and that it would be a perfect time to visit.

I was jumpy. The more I thought about it, the more I had become adamant about *not* going with Patrick to South Side Junior High School. My parents knew that I was afraid I'd be made fun of there. But I was also worried about not being able to keep up with the teachers and students in each class.

Perhaps I had purposely emphasized that part to my parents. However, it would have been tough enough transitioning into junior high school as a hearing student. To do it now, after being deaf for such a short while, seemed impossible.

"You guys sure it doesn't cost money for me to go here?" I asked. They'd told me the state sent money to this school and other schools like it. I couldn't quite understand it. I had read on the website that if I decided to go to school here, I'd be living here. The state was going to pay for me to live away from home?

Mom turned around and signed: *No.* She smiled reassuringly.

It might not cost money, but it *was* an awfully long car ride.

I couldn't imagine what it would be like to be in a school where everyone was deaf or hard of hearing. Before becoming deaf, I'd never even realized schools like this existed.

Dad, Mom, Marie and I climbed out of the car. Marie held Mom's hand. She looked nervous. I kept flashing her smiles that she returned. I wanted her to know everything would be okay.

We wandered around the buildings closest to the parking lot. They were big red-brick buildings set fairly close together. There were small lawns between them, and sidewalks and trees. But what was going on inside of them? Were there a lot of students sitting in classrooms? Were the same things being taught as in normal schools?

Marie's eyes were wide, lips pursed. I knew that she, like me, had no idea what to think or what to expect. She slid the palm of one hand down the palm of the other. *Nice,* she signed.

I nodded in agreement, still looking around. It was kind of nice.

I kept looking around for more people. We had seen a handful of people when we first pulled in, but otherwise the place was pretty deserted. I wanted to see what the guys my age were wearing. I mean, did deaf people dress the same? Patrick and I usually wore baggy T-shirts, sneakers, and shorts from April until October if the weather was cooperative.

When I looked back, my father had stopped and seemed to be talking to a girl. I guess he was asking where Perkins Hall was—that was where we had been told to go once we arrived at the school. She looked like she might be about my age. She wore jeans and red high-tops. She had light blonde hair with a red streak that matched her sneakers, and blue eyes. She carried a thick black book under her arm. I saw gold writing on the front cover, and a guy with tattoos all over his face. The title looked something like *Art on the Edge.*

The girl shook her head. She pointed at her chest, then at her lips and to her ear. *I'm deaf,* she signed.

Dad looked at Mom, his cheeks turned red. He was clearly blushing. He signed *Sorry* by making a fist and rubbing it in circles against his heart. She smiled and shrugged.

He wrote something down on a pad of paper and showed the girl. Then he held up his finger and wiggled back and forth: *Where?*

The girl smiled. She pointed toward one of the large brick houses. It was lavished with big windows and shutters—had it been nighttime and foggy out, I'd have sworn Perkins Hall was a haunted house. Then the girl looked at me and smiled. I felt my lips curl into a half smile. For whatever reason, she seemed to sense I was deaf. Her hands began to move quickly and I realized she was talking to me using sign language.

I shook my head apologetically. *Slowly, I'm learning to sign.*

She pointed at me. She pointed at her ear, at her lips, and then she brushed the tip of that finger up her lips a few times. She held up her thumbs, raised one, then the other, in that teeter-totter motion.

It took a minute for me to recognize the signs she used and then switch them around into English inside my brain. She had literally signed: *Deaf, hearing, which one?* But if you translate it from ASL into English, she was asking, *Are you deaf, or can you hear?*

I signed: *Deaf.*

She signed the letter "H" with both hands, pointing the first and middle fingers, thumbs tucked away. Then she tapped the middle finger side of the right hand across the index finger side of the left, making an "X." She wanted to know my name.

Marco, I spelled.

She spelled *Samantha.*

I nodded. I had no idea what else to say, what else to spell.

Dad tapped me on the shoulder, softly, and showed me his watch.

Samantha clapped her hands. I knew the sign. It meant *school.* She held out both hands, palms up, then in an arc, moved them down a few inches from where they hand been. It meant *here.* I figured she wanted to know if I'd be coming to school here.

Maybe, I signed.

She made a fist with her thumb across her fingers forming the letter "S" in sign language. She held the *S* up to the right corner of her mouth and wiggled it slightly, back and forth. She signed: *Me sign name.*

I had no idea what a *sign name* was, but I repeated the action.

Samantha looked a little startled and pulled a pager out of her front pocket. She showed it to me quickly. Words were typed out on the small flip-up monitor.

She held up the pager and then acted like the thing was trying to jump out of her hand. *Vibrates*, she spelled and smiled at us. That was how she knew she'd been paged. She signed: *I've got to go.* The way her hands moved fascinated me, like she really knew what she wanted to say and didn't have to think of each word before she signed it. I liked watching her fingers bend and straighten as her wrists pivoted and twisted. Smooth. Would it ever get that easy for me?

She touched the tips of her fingers to her chin with one hand and then clapped the back of that hand into the palm of the other. *Good.* She flicked the middle finger off her chin out and away from her. *Luck.* She waved goodbye and walked away.

I watched her until she walked into the building across from Perkins Hall. She was only the second deaf person I had ever met. My ASL teacher was the first. But that didn't count; she was a teacher.

As we walked toward Perkins Hall, Marie skipped in front of me and blew me kisses. Then she scolded me playfully, rubbing her fingers together as if they were sticks and she was trying to start a fire. She pointed at me, then repeated Samantha's sign name. I waved her away, but I couldn't help smiling. It would be cool to think I'd made a new friend.

CHAPTER 16

erkins Hall was nothing like I expected. It looked like some big old house that had been turned into offices. A huge staircase led upstairs to what looked like bedrooms. Big, gold-framed portraits hung on wallpapered walls. The doors were almost twice as tall as any doors I'd ever seen before, and most were kept open by wedges of wood shoved underneath. As we walked toward the reception area, I would have bet the floors were squeaking and moaning beneath the thick carpets.

A woman behind a desk greeted us with a salute. I saw my father say something to her. The lady motioned for us to sit in the chairs lining one of the walls. A moment later, a door opened and a woman who was tall enough to play professional basketball came out of an office.

She also greeted us with a salute. Then she fingerspelled her name: Nancy Funnel. Her lips moved when she spelled. We each fingerspelled our names. I wondered if she was talking and signing at the same time. I signed: *Are you deaf?*

No, she signed. *You sign well.*

Thank you, I signed. She wore her black hair down around her shoulders and was dressed in a dark blue shirt and tan slacks. Ms. Funnel led my family to her office and closed the door. Instead of stuffy portraits in gold frames hanging on her walls, she had a bunch of paintings of people's hands—hands in action—surrounded by lots of color. This lady had weird taste in art... I stared at one of the pictures, and suddenly understood it. I shook my head. The hands, side by side, had the first fingers pointing up, and the blurred motion made it look like the hands took turns pointing up to the sky. It was the sign for stars. At the end of each fingertip was a star. Awesome.

You like this? Ms. Funnel signed.

I nodded. "I see what it is, or what it says. It's hard to explain."

I know what you mean, she signed.

Marie stood next to me. She repeated the sign for stars. *Cool*, she signed.

I put a hand on Marie's shoulder as Ms. Funnel motioned for us to sit in the chairs around her desk. Marie sat next to me, moving her chair closer to me. I gave her a wink. She tried to wink back, but just ended up blinking with both eyes.

Ms. Funnel looked at me as she signed. I asked her to sign the words again. Some I understood, but others I could not pick up.

She tried again more slowly: *You'll see me sign as I talk. It is polite to sign in front of deaf people so they understand that you do know how to sign.*

I nodded. *Okay*, my hands replied.

She continued to sign and occasionally I asked her to repeat some things. Though she moved her hands carefully, she was using signs I wasn't familiar with. I was so busy concentrating that I had no idea what she was saying.

Dad wrote for a moment and showed me the tablet. *We have an appointment with Dr. Stein later this morning.*

I nodded. "Who is that? Why do we have to meet with a doctor?" The static sound was back, and louder than usual. I used a fingertip to swipe around inside my ear. It did absolutely nothing to stop the hissing.

He meets with all students, she signed. *You will like him.*

I wasn't sure I'd like talking with some doctor, but I wasn't ready to jump to any conclusions.

Dad, who sat next to me, wrote something down. He turned the pad so I could see what he wrote as he asked Ms. Funnel the question. *Does the school year run differently?*

Though Ms. Funnel continued to sign while she spoke, it helped me to read the notes my father wrote. Her signing was lively and graceful—even more so than the teacher at the high school. I was impressed at how easy she made the language look. I guess I thought that the classes we took at the high school—and all the time I spent studying—had made me something of an expert. Watching Samantha, and now Ms. Funnel, however, made it clear what a beginner I really was. I took a deep breath and exhaled. Everyone looked over at me. *Excuse me*, I signed.

I looked at the tablet when Dad had finished. *Same school calendar as other schools. Same class courses*, Dad had written. *All kids go home for summer. Summer school classes started after the 4th of July and finish by the middle of Aug.*

Some older students spend summers helping staff with younger students. Students move back in on the first day of school.

Mom raised her hand. She had a question. *Move back in?* she signed.

I tried to focus on Ms. Funnel's hands and I caught some of her answer, but still had to read what Dad had written: *150 students. Most do not live on campus. Most are day students. A lot of students live here Monday through Friday in dorms. Go home on weekends. NY State has only 8 schools for the deaf. Our school is the closest in about an 80-mile radius. When the school first opened, students almost never went home. Students used to live here year round. More recently, kids started going home weekends, holidays, and for summer break.*

I saw Mom put her hand was on Dad's leg like she was surprised. I could tell from my mother's expression that she didn't like what she was hearing. Dad wrote something down and showed me. It was what Mom had asked. *What about our son? Would he have to live here?*

Dad wrote down Ms. Funnel's answer: *Have to? No. We encourage family unity, as long as it's possible for a child to live at home. You drove from Batavia. That's a long drive. Campus closes at 6 p.m. on Fridays. Kids go home for the weekend and campus reopens Mondays. Classes start at 8:30 a.m. Could you manage driving your son and picking him up each day?*

I looked at Dad. He shrugged, but I knew the answer. It wasn't possible. Dad worked closer to Buffalo, which was in the opposite direction of Rochester. Besides, Mom needed to be home in the morning to put Marie on the bus and home at the end of the day to get her off the bus.

Why send Marco here, rather than to a school back home? Dad showed me the question he'd asked.

Ms. Funnel signed for a while. Her hands and her lips kept moving. Dad wrote quick points while she spoke: *Marco* should *be around other deaf people. A mainstream school is great for those who can hear. RSD has sports like soccer and basketball, clubs like chess and photography. There's a recreation center, student government, you name it. All of it is geared toward deaf and hard-of-hearing students.*

Mom and Dad nodded their heads. Ms. Funnel continued while Dad wrote: *Marco will work with a sign language specialist. One-on-one and class lessons. He will learn sign language from other students. Students teach each other better than instructors do. Marco will not be in the minority.*

Dad wrote: *What about class sizes?*

Ms. Funnel smiled. *Class sizes range from four to twelve students. Any more questions?*

I looked at Mom. I suspected she had more worries, but might wait to get Ms. Funnel alone before addressing them. I remembered the first time I slept over at Patrick's house—I was, like, five years old. Mom drove me over and chatted forever with Patrick's mother while Patrick and I stood in the living room. Finally we went off to play, but I could still hear my mother talking from Patrick's bedroom. Mom asked so many questions and said so many embarrassing things. Make sure he goes to the bathroom before falling asleep. What did she think? I was going to wet the bed? If he wants to come home, call me, I'll come pick him up—it doesn't matter what time it is. Did she think I was going to have some nightmare and need to go home in the middle of the night?

That had been a long time ago, but suddenly I found myself wondering if I would ever sleep over at Patrick's again.

Ms. Funnel tapped me on the shoulder. *Any questions?*

"What is a sign name?" I asked.

She shook her head. *You sign to me.*

I didn't make eye contact with her, instead, I concentrated on the way I shaped my hands when signing. *What is a sign name?* I felt my face heat up. She was so good at signing. What if she couldn't understand me?

Ms. Funnel smiled. I guess she was pleased with my question. *A nickname,* she fingerspelled her reply.

I met a Samantha, I signed then demonstrated to Ms. Funnel the sign name Samantha had shown me.

Exactly. See, it is easier to use a sign name than to fingerspell someone's name. Ms. Funnel signed. *Samantha, yes. She takes extra art classes during the summer.* Ms. Funnel used a combination of signing and fingerspelling.

What's my sign name?

That's up to your friends, Ms. Funnel signed. *You wouldn't give yourself a nickname, would you?*

I might have, but I didn't say anything.

Dad pointed a finger in the air, as if saying he had a question. Back to business. He fumbled with signing then shook his head, discouraged. He wrote: *If we decide to enroll Marco, what do we need to do?*

How silly and clumsy did we look to her, I wondered, with the way we goofed at signing and fingerspelling? I could see the hint of a smile in Ms. Funnel's expression. I didn't think she was laughing at us, though. It wasn't a mocking smile. It resembled something maybe more like pride—like maybe she was pleased to see us working with what we'd learned, even if we were stumbling. She signed: *There is a lot of paperwork. We'll need to work with your school district to get approval for Marco to attend classes here.*

Ms. Funnel must have seen a defeated look on my mom's face. She continued signing: *Relax. That's my job. What we should do is get started on filling out forms before you leave today. It sometimes takes a while before the state sends approval. And if Marco decides not to attend, that is okay, too.*

My parents both looked at me. I saw it. They might not think I did, but I saw how horrified they were as they sank exasperatedly into their chairs.

CHAPTER 17

I followed my family as Ms. Funnel led us across campus to another building. I still had to concentrate on walking, and I felt a little lightheaded. Though I hadn't used the cane in a while, a part of me knew I still needed it at times. Another part of me knew that even if I brought it, I wouldn't have used it. Everyone would stare.

When Ms. Funnel stopped to point out different buildings on campus, I didn't really pay attention. I watched two boys kick-dribble a soccer ball across the lawn, passing it back and forth until they rounded a corner. What would it be like living here, away from home? The brick buildings looked nothing like my house. Maybe I'd end up feeling more like a patient than a student. It would be tough enough leaving my family at home, and what about Whitney? What would she do without me?

I did not want to go to junior high at home, but neither did I want to leave home. But wasn't this like being a college student? They moved away from home and lived at school. This was the same thing, wasn't it?

None of those college kids were deaf.

Maybe deaf kids didn't even go to college.

What kinds of jobs could deaf people get anyway?

They? No. *I...* We.

What kinds of jobs can *we* get, anyway?

We couldn't become pilots. How would we hear the controllers telling us where to land a plane? We couldn't become doctors. How would we understand patients telling us what or where it hurt? We couldn't become lawyers. How would we convince a jury our client was innocent if they didn't know how to sign? We couldn't become police officers. How would we be able to hear a call coming in on the police radio? We couldn't become firefighters. If we went into a burning building, searching for people, how would we hear them calling for help?

And I knew I couldn't become a professional baseball player, either.

I was taken aback when we stopped outside the door of a Dr. Steve Stein's office. Under his nameplate it read: *Psychologist.* "I thought this doctor was going to give me a physical," I said. "Why do I have to see a psychologist?"

Families meet with the doctor at the end of a school tour, Ms. Funnel signed.

"It's not just because I'm new to deafness?" Sometimes talking was just easiest.

I guess she understood that, because she didn't make me sign. *No, not at all. He is just going to talk with you, ask some questions. And he will give you a chance to ask him questions, too.*

What did I know about psychologists? Nothing. People called them shrinks—*head* shrinks. That did not make me feel all warm and fuzzy inside. What kind of questions would he ask? What kind of answers did he expect? What kind of questions was *I* supposed to ask?

I watched Ms. Funnel knock on the door. My mind strained to hear the sound that her knuckles made as she rapped the solid wood—I couldn't detect a thing. She opened the door to a large office with a green carpet and book-lined shelves. Though his desk seemed piled with clutter, the doctor looked relaxed and comfortable amidst the jumbles of papers.

The Lippas? Dr. Stein spelled. *Hello!* He stood up from behind his desk. He was tall, but a few inches shorter than Ms. Funnel. He had thick, wavy gray hair. He wore a button-down shirt with the sleeves rolled halfway up to his elbow. He also had on jeans and sneakers. I wouldn't expect a doctor to be dressed this way, but I liked it. After shaking hands with each of us, he signed, *Have a seat, please.*

Marie and I sat between our parents at the small round table in the center of the doctor's office. Dr. Stein, still sitting, wheeled the chair from his desk over to the table with his feet. He seemed to talk and sign at the same time, like Ms. Funnel had done... as *I* sometimes did, as well.

I saw you look at my clothes. Summer dress code, he signed. *But I try to get away with not wearing a tie as often as possible.* He laughed.

I laughed, too. A little.

Dr. Allen called, told me you were coming. I am sure all of you have questions, he signed.

I watched as Mom and Dad and even Marie began talking to the doctor. Though Dr. Stein kept looking at me, I was left out of the conversation. I let it go on for as long as I could. I stood up. That got everyone's attention. "I can wait outside."

Your family was telling me they like the school, Dr. Stein signed. *How about you?*

"How about me?" The room felt like it might be getting smaller. It seemed hotter now than a moment ago and was getting even hotter by the second. "You're having fun. Don't worry about me."

Marco? Dad spelled. His combination of sign language and body expressions couldn't be mistaken. *Don't be rude,* it said.

"What is this? I don't need to see a psychologist. I'm deaf, not crazy." I didn't want to blow my chances of being accepted at this school, but how come no one told me sooner that I would have to talk with a shrink?

Please, sit down, Dr. Stein signed. *No one said you're crazy.*

"No one has to." I hoped my voice was quiet, just above a whisper. I didn't want to yell.

Dr. Stein must have asked for time alone with me because Mom, Dad, and Marie stood up and walked out of the office.

"What?" I said to the doctor.

Dr. Stein signed: *What's wrong with talking to me?*

"I'm not crazy."

Of course you are not crazy. But maybe you feel angry? Are you angry?

"No."

Sounds like you could be a little *angry.*

"Well, I'm not."

Why aren't you? I'd be, he signed.

This stopped me. "You'd be angry?"

Of course.

"I guess I'm a little ticked." I looked around the office at everything, at *anything* to avoid making eye contact with the doctor. I liked his globe. The ones in school were plain painted balls. His was made of a variety of shiny, textured rocks that made up the oceans and bodies of land.

Why?

"Why? Because I lost my hearing."

Dr. Stein picked up a yellow legal pad and wrote: *You didn't lose your hearing. That makes it sound as if you can find it again, as if you'd acted irresponsibly in the first place. You, Marco, became deaf.*

I read what the doctor had written and only shrugged.

What do you think of the school?

"I like it," I said. "I guess."

The doctor's forearm moved as he scratched down more words on the pad. *So you're considering coming here in the fall?*

"Ms. Funnel is going to start the paperwork," I said. "In case I decide I want to come here."

In September, come see me? We can talk. Sound good?

I nodded. "Yeah. I guess."

The doctor wrote for a while then slid the legal pad over to me. *It's OK to feel angry, or sad. You did lose something when you became deaf. It has changed your life. But it's up to you, Marco, to make the change a positive one.*

Easier said than done, I wanted to say. After all, he could hear. What did he know? Instead, I just grumbled. "Sure."

CHAPTER 18

P atrick and I lounged near the door, looking into my yard. The sun was brutal, sitting like a fireball in a cloudless sky, making it too hot to do much of anything other than sit on the backdoor step. Whitney found shade by the maple tree at the side of the yard. I'd given her a bowl of water, but she looked too hot and tired to raise her head high enough for a drink.

Patrick's mitt was out on the lawn, next to his bike. My mitt was in the house, in my room, and my bike was in the garage. I had no intention of playing catch or going for a ride. When I told Patrick this, I expected him to leave. Instead, he sat on the step with me. This surprised me. Since that baseball game weeks ago, I had not been much fun to be around. Patrick kept coming over to see if I wanted to do anything. I either avoided him, or did like I was doing now—nothing.

Summer's going to be over soon, he wrote on the pad he'd brought over with him.

"Goes by kind of quick," I agreed.

Your mom says you got accepted to another school. I noticed he made less spelling mistakes than at the beginning of the summer.

"A school for deaf kids," I said. I almost added, *like me,* but it was obvious, so I didn't.

Are you sure you can't go to junior high with me? He stared at me as I read what he wrote.

"We had to do a lot of paperwork in order for me to go to this school. If I go to our school first, I lose my spot. And then if I don't feel comfortable there, I'm stuck," I explained, speaking slowly, concentrating on listening for the sound of my own voice. "Since I got in at RSD, I can go there next week. If I don't like it, I can leave and go to our junior high with no problem."

So you are just trying out this other school? he wrote.

"Exactly."

I hope you don't like it there.

I almost asked why, but I knew the answer. We'd been best friends since forever. "It's not like we won't see each other," I said. I looked over at Whitney. She seemed to know I was focusing on her. Her tail lazily slapped at the grass, but just once. "Look, I know I'm not much fun to be around . . ."

You're my best friend. I don't care what we do, but I miss hanging out with you, he wrote.

"You do? Why? I can't play baseball. Riding a bike scares me to death. You have to write down everything. What fun is any of that?"

He underlined "best friend" on the note he'd written.

"Want to go play some video games?"

He wrote then showed me the pad of paper. *Now you're talking!*

When Patrick left, I went into the garage and picked up a soccer ball and headed out into the backyard. I set the ball down and looked around to make sure no one was watching me.

I wasn't really a soccer player. I didn't know much about the game, except that you are supposed to kick the ball into the other team's net. Thinking this would be a good way to work on my balance and coordination, I gave the ball a kick with the side of my foot. It rolled out a few feet. I stepped toward it, kicked it again a little harder. It rolled a little further. I trotted toward it, kicking it, dribbling down the length of the yard, careful not to go too fast.

My toe jabbed at the ground. My arms shot out, but before I could break my fall my stomach smashed onto the ball. The air rushed out of my lungs. I rolled off the ball and lay on my back, panting.

The sky wasn't as blue as it had been earlier. There was a slight breeze stealing some of the heat from the sun, and small cottony clouds were scattered about and slowly floating by.

Why me? What did I ever do to deserve this? Wasn't the world filled with bad people? Robbers? Murderers? So, why did this have to happen to me?

When I sat up, my head felt like a helium-filled balloon. I planted my palms on the grass to steady myself. I waited a moment and then got into a squatting position. I stood up, ready to lose my balance, ready to fall down, ready for lightheadedness.

Instead, I was fine.

Fine. What was fine about me? That I could stand without getting dizzy? That was fine?

Soccer was a stupid sport. Moments ago, I'd taken it easy. This time I kicked at the ball using every bit of strength and energy I had. My foot sailed past the ball without so much as skimming it. Before I knew what had happened, I was on my back beside the dumb ball, gasping for air again.

I wasn't sure about using soccer as a way to work on my balance anymore. It had seemed like a good idea a minute ago. Finally, I put the ball away and went into the house.

Dinner, Mom signed. She stood in front of the sink by the window and put potholder mitts on. Then she poured steaming water into a plastic strainer, and a huge wad of spaghetti plopped into the strainer. She took off the mitts and signed: *Chicken parm, your favorite!*

"Not hungry. I want to go upstairs and rest for a little while." My excuse for everything.

Mom nodded like she understood. She didn't argue. She didn't try to convince me to join the family at the table. She let me go. That was actually pretty cool of her.

I figured that if she had been working at the sink by the window, she'd probably seen me kicking the soccer ball. And if she saw that, she saw how terrible I was—and felt bad for me.

I actually *did* feel tired. More and more lately, sleeping was becoming a problem. At night, I felt anxious and nervous about leaving home and going away to a new school; I found myself constantly tossing and turning.

I lay down on my bed on top of the covers. I folded my hands behind my head and closed my eyes. Though I'd told my mother I wasn't hungry, the truth was I was starving. I didn't expect to fall asleep, but without knowing it, I did.

I began having the same dream I'd had a hundred times before, ever since I got really into baseball. In it, I'm pitching in a game. It doesn't matter what team I'm on or who we're playing. Instinctively, I know the facts. It is the bottom of the ninth inning. Bases loaded. Two outs. Two strikes. Three balls. I have to smile—even in the dream—it's a do-or-die situation.

On the mound, I'm sweating so much I look like someone just popped a water balloon over the top of my head. As I get ready for the wind up—I've decided to throw the elusive curve ball—I stop.

This part was new to the dream. I never stopped before. The crowd is usually cheering me on, chanting my name, screaming and hollering so loudly that I can't even hear my own thoughts. But that's just it. That's why I stopped.

Not only can I *not* hear the crowd cheering me on, I can't even hear my own thoughts. And when I strain to see the people in the stands from the pitcher's mound—everyone is signing at me.

Go Marco! Strike him out! You're the best!

I'm completely deaf. Even in my dreams.

CHAPTER 19

SEPTEMBER

In the morning, I would be leaving for the Rochester School for the Deaf. I wasn't sure how to feel. Everyone I knew would be going to Batavia's junior high. But I wasn't like all my old friends. Besides, except for Patrick, not many other kids came over to ask if I wanted to hang out. All they wanted to do was play baseball, anyway, and I was so over the stupid game. It didn't matter. A hundred kids could have stopped by. It wouldn't have changed a thing. Not one thing.

In my room, I grabbed the unused pizza box from under my bed, and set it beside me. Inside, stapled sheets of aluminum foil protected my collection. The baseball cards were stacked in rows and rows inside, arranged alphabetically by team, and then alphabetically by player.

I didn't need to fish around to find my favorite card. I picked Hoyt Wilhelm out and stared at the back of the card for a moment, taking in the stats that I already knew by heart. Wilhelm, who retired in 1972, was known as the "knuckleball master." He appeared in 1,070 games—more than any other pitcher in Major League Baseball history. He had 123 relief wins, and was a relief pitcher in 1,028 games, for a total of 1,870 innings. Despite having fewer than 150 wins, he was the first relief pitcher inducted into the Hall of Fame. He always gave his all, even though he was rarely the starting pitcher. The only thing that could impress me more is if he'd also been deaf.

I knew I'd never play professional baseball. What team would draft a deaf player? I couldn't even play out the rest of this year's baseball season. The few more times that I had kicked a soccer ball around in the backyard, I'd fallen flat on my face. Any hope at an athletic career was over.

My cheeks heated up. A part of me wanted to throw out the entire collection. The feeling the cards had once inspired in me was dead. Now I just got a scary, hollow feeling when I looked at them. After a moment I slid the box back under the bed. It had taken me a long time to collect those cards; I shouldn't do anything rash.

I took a suitcase out of the closet. The card collection might not be going with me to my new school, but I needed to pack other essential things.

The intake process, as the school called it, had seemed endless. Ms. Funnel had had us fill out mounds of paperwork. Then most of the forms needed to be submitted to the state for approval. After that, there were medical examinations and placement tests, until finally it was all over. The Rochester School for the Deaf was now going to be *my* school.

Dad had arranged to arrive late the next day for work. Marie would miss a bit of her first day of fourth grade. In the morning, we planned to stop for a big pancake breakfast in Rochester before arriving at the school.

I picked up the sign language dictionary my mother had bought me. I knew I needed to pack it. It was like a regular dictionary, except next to each word was a written description of how to sign the word, not a definition. There were also drawings of a person performing the sign. I was definitely bringing my computer with me. The Internet had awesome lessons on signing that beat trying to figure out hand motions from illustrations in a book. Lately, I spent a lot of time holed up in the bathroom practicing, watching my technique in the mirror, and trying to make my fingers move more quickly.

The bedroom door opened. My fingers rolled into my palms. I didn't feel like talking. Marie stuck her head in and gave me a look, sort of asking permission to enter the room. My hands relaxed. I waved her in.

She sat down on the bed and I joined her.

Marie set down the folded piece of white construction paper she'd held in her hands and held up her right hand. For a moment she just stared at it as if it were about to perform tricks.

I watched my sister sign that she'd made a drawing for me.

It just amazed me how good she was at signing. Her hands moved with such ease, though I rarely saw her study. "You do a real good job signing, Marie."

Thank you. She handed me the construction paper.

I didn't know what to expect. When I unfolded the paper, I sure wasn't prepared for the impact her artwork would have on me.

It was a portrait of me. She had made my hair look bristled like an army brush cut, my forehead creased, and my eyes big and round. The elongated nose she'd drawn resembled a ski slope and my mouth consisted of fat lips. I couldn't tell if I was smiling or not.

That was interesting.

This me, I signed.

She nodded.

I stood up and went over to look in the mirror. It really did sort of look like me.

I turned and showed Marie, holding the drawing up next to my face.

She smiled—then giggled. I sat back down and tickled her. She squirmed this way and that, trying to get free.

I stopped tickling her then because I was missing the sound of her laugh.

She looked up at me. Her cheeks were red from laughing, but her smile was gone. She didn't have to ask to know what I was feeling.

Sitting back down, I noticed the background in the drawing. Marie had drawn the symbol of the New York Yankees, the "Y" over the "N," in bold blue letters. I held out my hand, made a "Y" in ASL with the other. I then scraped the knuckles of the "Y" in the palm of the other, nice and fast. It meant *Yankees*.

At the bottom she had written, in careful lettering, *I Love You*. Next to it, she had drawn a hand saying it in sign language—the hand showed the thumb out with the first finger and the pinkie up. The two middle fingers pointed down toward the wrist.

"I love it," I said. "I really do—it's beautiful!"

Marie took the picture out of my hands and turned it over. On the back she'd written, *I'm going to miss you*. She wrapped her arms around me and started crying.

We were brother and sister—we didn't hug. We argued. We squabbled. We tried to annoy each other but, come to think of it, I couldn't remember us bickering since I got sick. I hugged her back. "I love you, too." I don't think I'd ever told my sister that. I hugged her even tighter. "I'm really going to miss you."

⟨⤙⟩

Later, Dad walked into my room. *Packed?* he signed.

"By the door." I watched Dad look at the few suitcases and the backpack.

Leave early tomorrow morning, he responded.

"Fine."

He looked around the room, then went over to the corner and picked up my baseball bat and mitt. *These?*

"'These, what?'" Pretending not to know what he meant, I sat down on the bed and folded my arms.

Bringing them with you?

"Why bring them? I don't play baseball anymore." I pushed back on the bed, and backed my body up against the headboard. "Leave them here."

But why? he signed.

"I *don't* want them, Dad. They're not coming with me." I stared at him, knowing I had raised my voice some—I wasn't yelling—I just wanted him to understand that there was nothing to discuss. I didn't want to be forced to bring a bat and mitt with me when I knew I'd never use them.

What if you want to play? he signed.

I got off the bed. "I won't."

I slung the backpack strap over my shoulder and picked up the suitcases, nearly losing my balance, but managing to steady my legs and keep hold of everything.

"I hate baseball." I walked out the door.

CHAPTER 20

I opened my eyes. No sunlight filled the room. I looked at the clock: 5:00 a.m. I could close my eyes, rest some more. I *could*—but I knew I wouldn't be able to fall back to sleep. Instead, I rolled out of bed, got ready for the big day and headed out the door, ready to pile into the car for the drive to Rochester.

When I got outside I stopped and shook my head. "Hey, Patrick! What are you doing up this early?"

He was wearing new jeans and sneakers and holding a paper and pen with him, like he usually did when he came over. *Couldn't let you take off without saying bye*, he wrote. *First day of school for me, too. I'd have had to get up sooner or later, anyway.*

I read what he wrote and laughed. I wished I could hear myself laugh. I couldn't even remember what it sounded like anymore. "Thanks."

And I wanted to give you this. He pulled a brand new Yankees baseball cap from his backpack, and handed it over. The one I had was beyond old and comfy. It was worn out and a bit embarrassing to wear.

I felt funny taking the cap after the outburst with my father last night. But hey, best I could tell, the Yankees had done nothing to me, so why should I hold my deafness against them? I tried it on. "Cool, man. Thanks!"

Sure. I better go, he wrote after noticing how my family was frantically circling the car.

I wish I had thought to get him something. My brain searched for anything I might have in my bag, anything that I could give to him, but nothing came to mind. "Maybe we can do something this weekend?"

Sounds good. Have fun at school.

"You, too!" We did our handshake. It was different this time. Slower. It felt like it meant more that way, instead of rushing through it.

When we pulled out of the driveway, Patrick stayed on the sidewalk waving. I waved back. I had known for weeks that we wouldn't be going to school together, and I had known it would be weird, but until right that instant, it just didn't seem real. I watched him leave and knew he was thinking the same thing.

⚬⚬⚬

We arrived in Rochester early, which was part of Dad's plan. The restaurant where we stopped for breakfast had a big parking lot. Inside, everything was brown and green. The booths were brown leather. It was nothing like the small family-owned diner at home. Food didn't even smell the same. The servers wore green aprons. There had to be thirty booths along the walls and as many tables in the center of the dining area. The place smelled of pancakes, maple syrup, bacon, and coffee.

We sat in a back-corner booth. It was the first time since I'd become deaf that we'd gone out to eat as a family. I was able to see everyone in the place. When the waitress came to the table, everyone else ordered. I went last, concentrating on pronouncing each word correctly. Maybe I was slurring words or mumbling. How could I know? After ordering, I folded my menu and attempted to hand it to the waitress. Her lips moved. I couldn't tell what she said and I looked quickly at my dad.

Dad spoke to the waitress with an apologetic look on his face. The waitress took the menu from me and opened the plastic-coated flaps. She pointed to the item I'd ordered: two eggs scrambled, rye toast, and a glass of orange juice. "Bacon, please," I added. "Not sausage."

When the waitress left, I scowled.

What? Dad signed.

"You told her I was deaf, didn't you?"

Dad threw his hands in the air.

Mom signed, *What should your father do? She asked you a question.*

They were right. What did I expect? People were going to need to know I was deaf. I didn't know why I thought I could keep it a secret. Why was I ashamed of being deaf?

After eating, Marie sat up front with Dad because Mom wanted to sit in back with me. She held my hand, her thumb massaging my knuckles. I couldn't look at her. Instead, I nestled in close until she wrapped an arm around my shoulder and held me tight. The thought of being without my family frightened me more than I wanted to admit. The idea of living alone on a campus where I only knew the lady from admissions made me turn cold.

The Yankees ball cap felt tight and stiff on my head. It needed to be broken in. Getting caught in a heavy downpour was one of the best ways to baptize a ball cap, but…

Mom squeezed my hand, letting me know she wanted my attention. She pointed at me and asked if I was okay.

I nodded. I was afraid that if I said anything, I would start to cry and not be able stop. We were driving in the car on the way to my new school. I didn't want to be bawling in my mother's lap like a baby. I wanted to be brave for my family. "Fine," I managed.

Nervous? Mom spelled.

"Some."

You don't have to stay, Mom signed. *We can work with our schools back home.*

I shook my head and shrugged, as if to say: *We're already here, too late now.*

And it felt as if it *were* too late. What I really wanted was to scream for Dad to turn the car around and take us home. But I didn't.

It was around 7:00 a.m. when Dad pulled into the school parking lot.

Everything was different now. Everything.

CHAPTER 21

ancy Funnel stood waiting for us by the admissions building. She gave a big wave as we approached, making sure we saw her.

I figured we must look completely out of place, like a family on vacation somewhere for the first time. Dad carried the suitcases, Mom held bags from the grocery store, Marie had my pillow slung over her shoulder the way Santa Claus carried a bag of toys, and I walked a few steps behind, bowed under my backpack.

Good morning, Ms. Funnel signed and wasted no time as she led us past the admissions building to Willis Hall. *This is the boys' dorm room. Younger kids on the first level, older kids upstairs,* she continued as she led us up a staircase.

An easel holding a chalkboard displayed a list of chores telling who was responsible for what. Someone had to take out the trash, someone else had to sweep the hall floors, while someone else was responsible for keeping the lounge area clean. But above the lists, in big colorful balloon letters, someone had written: *WELCOME, MARCO LIPPA.*

Mom looked at me and smiled. I tried to smile back, but inside me a big space had just opened up. Seeing those words should have made me feel welcome. Instead, they made me feel hollow again. I was the new kid, the outsider. I would be living here, away from home, away from my family.

Ms. Funnel went all the way to the end of the hall. I noticed some of the doors on the floor were open. I looked into the big rooms as I walked by, noting the plain white walls, the beds and dressers. The room Ms. Funnel led us into was no different—bare walls and two beds, two dressers, and two nightstands split down the middle in a mirror image. The bed by the window was made with a Star Wars bedspread. Books and a box of tissue paper were on the dresser beside it. I set my backpack down onto the other one. *This mine?* I signed.

Ms. Funnel nodded, made a fist and shook it up and down. *Yes.* She explained that I had an eight-year-old roommate, Kyle.

"Eight?" I said and used my hands, touching my middle finger to my thumb—the sign for the number eight. That would be like rooming with my sister! Though my sister's cool, it didn't mean I wanted to team up with some other peewee kid.

Ms. Funnel nodded. *He can't wait to meet you.*

I'll bet. He'd be getting a big brother out of the deal, while I'd be getting stuck with a babysitting job—only without any pay.

Mom didn't waste any time. She took the suitcase from Dad, unzipped it and unpacked the clothes onto the bed, then began to sort and fill the dresser drawers. Next, she set to work on the grocery bags, emptying onto the bed cream-filled cupcakes, bags of chips, boxes of raisins, some bubble gum, and packets of dried apples and apricots.

This made Ms. Funnel laugh. *Kids don't go hungry,* she told her. *The fridge is in the lounge, down the hall. I'll help you put that stuff in there, if you'd like.*

Mom touched a hand to her heart. I couldn't see what she said, but I assumed it was the I'm-his-mother-I-worry bit. She performed this for my teacher on the first day of kindergarten, first grade, second grade—she's done it every year. I knew how lucky I was to have her as my mom, but it was still hard not to be embarrassed by her.

The lounge also has a small kitchen table, a stove and microwave, Ms. Funnel signed.

I realized Marie was just standing in the doorway, shifting her weight from one foot to the other. With her hands behind her back, she stared at the ceiling, at the floor and at the walls.

"You like my new room?"

She pouted, but nodded, *Yes.*

I took the pillow from her and set it on the bed, unzipped the backpack and took out the picture Marie had drawn for me, along with a roll of tape. After I hung the picture over my dresser, I looked at Marie for approval.

She smiled and clasped her hands together. Her cheeks turned red.

I knelt beside her and opened my arms. She came into them, hugging me tightly. I hugged her back. Her tears wet through my shirt and felt cool on my skin.

"I need you to do me a favor." I hoped I was whispering.

Marie pulled out of the hug and looked me in the eyes. "I want you to take care of Whitney for me while I'm here at school, okay?" My throat burned from holding back my own tears. I really wanted to be brave for them so they wouldn't worry so much about me. They weren't making this easy. "She's going to need someone to walk her, and feed her, and make sure she has fresh water—every day."

Marie kept nodding that she could do it. Her lips quivered and tears streaked down her face. Then she hugged me again, wrapping her arms tightly around my neck. I looked up at Mom and Dad. They had an arm around each other. Both had tears in their eyes.

6∞9

When we stepped out of the dorm into the bright early morning sunlight, the school campus had been transformed. It was 8:00 a.m. and kids were everywhere—all different ages and sizes, boys and girls. Which ones would be in classes with me?

I noticed kids that looked my age grouped together, some carrying backpacks and others cradling books, walking toward one of the buildings. I saw parents leading younger children by the hand toward another building.

So young, Dad spelled.

"They're deaf, not sick," I snapped.

Not what I meant, Dad signed. *So young to be living away from home.*

The parking lot had been altered into a loop so cars could easily pull up and let kids out.

At the car, Dad pulled out his wallet and handed me money. *Enough?*

"Yeah, Dad." I brought my fingertips to my chin and lowered my hand. "Thank you."

Call us tonight, Mom signed, making a letter "Y" and holding her thumb to her ear and her pinkie to her mouth. Though the TTY was installed recently, we hadn't had an opportunity to use it yet.

When Mom, Dad and Marie finally got into the car, I was surprised to feel my mouth go dry. Knowing I was going to be living at school and actually doing it were two different things. As they drove away, I stood there waving and waving until I couldn't see them any longer, and then I stood just a moment more, my hand frozen in the air. My legs felt as if they'd turned to lead.

Standing alone at the edge of the parking lot I was not sure I remembered what I was to do next. I was supposed to go somewhere. Ms. Funnel had given me a map and a schedule, but… did she want me to come back and meet her? Or was I supposed to just head to a class?

I stuffed my hands into my pockets and slowly turned around, looking at the trees, the grass, and the buildings. There was still a smattering of kids going from here to there. Most everyone else seemed to have vanished. I knew classes would be starting soon.

Ms. Funnel stood by a tree waving at me. *Oh yeah*—I was supposed to meet with her! I walked over to where she stood. Ms. Funnel put an arm around my shoulder and we headed toward a long red-brick, rectangular-shaped building with a sign hanging over the door: Westervelt Hall. She opened the door for me. A row of vending machines lined one wall, while unusual art, depicting hands doing strange things in vibrant colors, hung on the others. It was different than the art that hung in Ms. Funnel's office. I'd never seen anything like it.

We passed through another doorway. On the left was the auditorium. We went up a few stairs on the right and then down a hall that led to the beginning rows of classrooms.

"How many kids here?" I asked and signed.

All together, one hundred and forty-five, Ms. Funnel signed. *Your classes will be on the third floor. We're going to meet your interpreter.*

Will I be going to classes this week?

Some. Mostly you will work more on signing, Ms. Funnel explained.

As we walked down the hall, I looked into the classrooms where students were sitting at desks. The walls were papered with colorful posters and fly-ers—so many bright colors advertising soccer tryouts, play auditions, the importance of reading, and lunch menus. There were also movie posters and magazine pages hung all over the place. I saw stocked bookshelves and globes hanging on their axes. Everything looked similar to the way it was at my old school.

I took a deep breath and exhaled. *Day One—ready or not, here I go.*

CHAPTER 22

M s. Funnel and I entered Mrs. Joyce Campbell's office—the nameplate outside the office door said so. Mrs. Campbell was going to be my interpreter. Her office was kind of small. Her desk sat by a window where the shades were drawn. In addition to the desk, she had some filled bookshelves and, in the center of the room, a round table with four chairs.

I smiled and extended my hand. "Hello." We clasped hands.

I felt funny signing in front of people I didn't know. It made me uncomfortable. Part of it was, I guessed, because I didn't think I was good enough at signing. The other part was that, every time I signed, I was admitting the truth to myself: I would never hear again.

Mrs. Campbell nodded and began signing. *Oral is good*. Like Ms. Funnel, she signed slowly. *Visual is good. Signing is good. We'll work more on all of this.*

She told me she was a retired city school teacher and worked at RSD as an interpreter because she was fluent in American Sign Language. She mostly worked with students who were four and five years old. I'm not sure why she was assigned to me. As long as I didn't get treated like a baby, I guess it didn't matter.

Mrs. Campbell was shorter than Ms. Funnel, but still pretty tall. She was thin, too. She wore her gray hair short and her glasses on a beaded necklace dangling in front of her. Her skin was dark, as if she'd spent all summer tanning under the sun.

It looks like you're in good hands, Marco, Ms. Funnel signed. *I'll be going back to my office, but if you need me, you know where I sit.* We shook hands goodbye.

Thank you. I watched Ms. Funnel leave. I placed an arm across my stomach as the muscles there tightened. I longed to be home. I thought I might get sick. It had only been five minutes and already I missed my family. How could this work? How could I ever learn to speak with my hands the way everyone else around here did?

You've been taking classes? Mrs. Campbell signed.

Yes, I signed back. She wore a constant smile, as if always reassuring me that this would all work out just fine. I wasn't sure I believed her. But right now she seemed to believe it. So I just went with that—taking as much comfort as possible from her smile.

You are doing very well.

Thank you. I practice a lot.

She nodded. *Ready to begin lessons with me?*

I took a deep breath. I wasn't, but what would be the point in telling her? I nodded as I signed, *Yes.*

She handed me pages that looked like they were photocopied from a book. Each page was split into two sections. The top had ten sentences in English. The bottom had ten sentences written out in ASL. At a glance, it looked like twenty completely different sentences.

She folded my sheet of paper in half, showing me only the sentences in English. She asked, *Sign these sentences in ASL.*

The first sentence in English was:

You played football in the morning, and played soccer in the afternoon, and now you are sick?

This was a fairly complicated sentence for me. There were a bunch of ASL rules I tried to remember in order to twist that sentence from English into ASL. One had to do with time.

Time comes first.

I signed, *Morning, you football played, afternoon you soccer played, now sick you?*

Mrs. Campbell smiled. *Very good. Okay. Try sentence number two.*

I read: *I watched the swimming competition.*

This one did not contain time. But the topic was swimming, and the topic was to come first.

In ASL I signed: *Swimming competition me watch.*

Close. She wrote something on a piece of paper and then showed it to me.

"When something is past tense," I read aloud, "like watched, or words ending in '-ed,' you need to end your sentence with the sign, 'finish.'" I looked up from the paper. "Using finish makes a word past tense?" I asked, not sure I understood.

She nodded. *Again.*

Swimming competition me watch finish, I signed.

Good. She smiled.

I thought about the next sentence, putting together everything I'd learned. You can place the time, *Saturday*, first or the subject, *movie*, first. Or, you can put the question, *want you*, at the beginning or at the end of the sentence.

I pursed my lips tight, and sighed through my nose as I shook my head.

This wasn't her fault. But it was kind of crazy. Why couldn't I just sign in plain, old *regular* English?

Just before noon she folded her hands and smiled. She placed the fingertips of her right hand near her lips. *Eat,* she signed, placing her right elbow on the palm of her left hand, keeping her right arm up, as if saying hello. *Noon,* she spelled.

She had been doing this all morning. Signing, spelling, and asking me to figure out what was going on. She called this a compound sign: two separate words used to make up one word. Eat and noon. "Lunch?" I asked.

Lunch, Mrs. Campbell signed, obviously pleased. *Company, or alone?*

I didn't know what to answer. I didn't want to eat lunch alone. Being in a room with deaf kids who could communicate easily with one another would be no different than if I'd gone to junior high back home. I'd still be left out, isolated. Still, I couldn't imagine taking a teacher with me to lunch.

It's okay, she signed. *If I were you, I'm not sure I'd want* me *tagging along, either.*

I raised my eyebrows, silently asking if she was sure.

Enjoy, she signed. *Be back before one.*

I held up a finger and shook it gently back and forth. *Where?*

Forrester Hall, she spelled. She used her finger like a voice, and gave me directions—moving it in the directions I needed to take to get to Forrester Hall.

Go out, go right, go straight, go right.

Thank you. I walked down the hall, toward an exit. Class might have gone fine, but I was feeling sick to my stomach about going to the cafeteria.

CHAPTER 23

E ntering Forrester Hall, I saw the cafeteria on my left and a familiar knot twisted in my gut. A line of students of all different ages disappeared into an area where food was served. More kids passed me, picked up trays off a nearby counter, then stood in line.

I took a tray then got in behind them and glanced around, trying not to be too obvious, and then I almost laughed—not because anything was funny. At my old school, the cafeteria was the noisiest place in the whole building. Even though lunch monitors wanted to keep everyone quiet, there was no getting around all the shouting, laughing, and screaming.

My ears mourned the silence, while at the same time, the visual chaos assaulted my eyes. The cafeteria was filled with kids slapping their palms on the tabletops to get the attention of their friends. One little girl, about six years old with half a sandwich in her mouth, walked over to a table and tapped another little girl on the shoulder; the two began signing before the first girl went back to her seat. I saw students signing to one another from across the room, laughing at something, a joke maybe.

The weird thing was, though there were a lot of kids around, the silence made the place seem deserted, like we were ghosts or spirits wandering around, haunting a school campus.

A tap on my shoulder startled me. I spun around. Two boys stood there. The Asian boy sneered and pointed toward the moving line. I was holding everyone else up. I formed a letter "A" with my right hand and made a small circle over my chest. *Sorry.*

I loaded my tray: pizza with pepperoni, fries drowning in catsup, and a soda with lots of ice. My old school had a cafeteria, but nothing like this. This was most definitely a perk! I paid using the meal card sent in the mail last week. Dad had made sure money was on it, but I didn't want to use up too much at once. As I tucked the card back into my wallet, I began the search for a place to eat.

The cafeteria was large and bright with big windows looking out onto the center of campus—green grass with picnic tables, some trees, and kids outside roaming about or playing. The cafeteria had lots of round tables and the room was about half-empty. Many of the kids were young enough to have an adult at the table helping cut up food or stick straws into drink boxes.

I saw empty chairs at most of the tables; a few kids that looked about my age sat at two of them. I wanted to sit with them, but there was no way I was just going to walk over and plunk myself down or ask if I could join them. What if someone told me to get lost? That was definitely not a way to begin my new life here. Just the thought of it made me sweat.

I spotted an empty table toward the back of the room. All eight chairs to myself. I sat down in one that allowed me to look around the room. Though I didn't want to stare, I *did* want to see what was going on. So, I picked up a french fry and focused on it as if it might be some baffling, marvelous new discovery before I stuffed it into my mouth.

Suddenly, a lunch tray appeared next to mine. I looked up.

Remember me? It was Samantha, the girl I met when I visited the school with my parents.

I made a fist, held it with my thumb near my lips and wiggled it and said, "Samantha."

She smiled, her eyes blinking slowly in a lazy, delighted way. *And you are Marco. How's school?*

Good.

May I sit? She pointed at the chair.

Sure. I didn't normally hang out with girls, but she seemed okay. I'd have preferred eating lunch with Patrick. Since that wasn't possible, Samantha would do. Besides, I liked the red streak in her hair. It was different. Girls in Batavia didn't do this.

After setting her art book down, she picked up a fistful of fries and crammed three into her mouth. Yeah, she definitely seemed all right.

What are you staring at?

I realized only then that I had been. *You're shirt.*

She held the fabric out at the shoulders so I could get a better look. Four guys in leathers leaning against a brick wall. "The Ramones" was spray painted across the top.

You like them?

Never heard of them. Are they a band? I signed.

Never heard of them? She signed. I knew she mocked my ignorance when her tongue stuck out of the corner of her mouth and she rolled her eyes. She laughed. *We are going to change that.*

I wanted to tell her it was kind of late. I was deaf. How was she going to change my *hearing* this band. I almost laughed.

What's so funny?

I shook my head. *Nothing.*

She shoved more fries into her mouth, nodded her head up and down, like these were the best fries ever.

I almost asked about the book, but felt my appetite come back, so I did the same with a few fries. She laughed.

Food's not bad. Her signing was a little fast, but I didn't want to ask her to slow down.

Not when you're starving. I laughed.

Another kid came over with a tray of food. Samantha smiled and waved a hello toward him. Then she introduced us. *This is Brian.*

He and I shook hands. *I'm Marco.*

He was African American and at least two inches taller than me. I noticed his New York Yankees T-shirt right away.

She signed to Brian, *Join us?*

He shook his head, set down his tray. *Can't. Meeting some guys to kick around the soccer ball.* He looked at me. *Nice meeting you. See you later.*

See you later, I signed.

Out of the corner of my eye I saw it. A french fry landed on top of Samantha's head. The table beside her silently exploded. The six boys seated there slapped down their hands on the table and threw their heads back—presumably in wild laughter.

Samantha shook her head and tried to smile as she picked the fry out of her hair. Unfortunately, the catsup blended with the streak. I couldn't tell how much was dye, and how much was condiment.

Without thinking, I took a fry off my plate and whipped it back at the table of kids. I don't know why I did it. Patrick and I always had little food fights during lunch. The cool thing was, no one knew about them. We'd target someone, and then I'd take a pea or something and whip it at that person. We kept score—I usually hit more targets than Patrick, so I got more points. The points meant nothing, really. It was just in fun. One time, someone caught on and threw a grilled cheese sandwich back at us. It hit me in the back. Patrick didn't hesitate. He took a blob of mashed potatoes and, using his spoon as a catapult, began one of the school's most memorable food fights of all time. He did that for me... but it was all in fun, and felt like everyone in school knew it. I was in a new school, though. Patrick wasn't here.

Two things happened simultaneously. One, the fry struck a boy in the face. Two, I realized the fry I'd sent flying was also covered in catsup. I closed my eyes for a moment and wished I could go back ten seconds in time to be given a chance *not* to do things the same way.

No such luck.

The kid jumped to his feet, wiping the catsup off his cheek and nose with a napkin. It was the same Asian kid who had been behind me in line. He looked even bigger now. He crumpled the napkin and dropped it on the floor as he marched toward my table.

He signed at me with lightning fast, angry hands. My eyes widened. I couldn't keep up. He was mad at me, that much I knew.

Samantha jumped out of her seat and stood in front of the kid.

They argued with their hands. You could see it in their tight facial expressions, their rolling eyes.

Words flew off fingertips. Her hand speed was no match for his.

I wanted to press my hands over my ears; even though the fighting was silent, it felt like a thundering ruckus. It looked like Samantha was keeping her cool, but the kid she was arguing with kept shaking his head and making faces.

The argument ended when Samantha pointed toward the door, telling him to go. He turned and glared at me. It was like a laser beam of anger shot out of his eyes. For a moment, I tried to stare right back at him, but I looked away first.

The last thing I wanted or needed was trouble, though it was probably too late to wish for that. What a way to kick off the new school year.

As he stormed off, he hit the back of an empty chair. It slid a few feet and collided with a table. Samantha watched him and his friends leave. She looked over at me, made a fist, and rubbed it over her chest in small circles. Her lips moved, as she signed: *You should not have done that.*

It's okay, I signed.

No. I mean, you really should not have done that. Eiji is not a nice kid. He likes to fight.

Oh. The bad feeling in my gut returned. *I see.*

She signed, *Here's my number... just in case.*

CHAPTER 24

fter lunch, the afternoon dragged. Mrs. Campbell reviewed the things we had practiced that morning.

Thankfully, class finally ended at precisely 3:30. In ASL, they don't say *finally*, they say, *PAH!* Which is like *Phew! Finally!* To do this, I twirled both index fingers once around by my temples, and ended the sign with the fingers pointing up and outward. I rolled my eyes, exaggerating the emphasis. When I signed this, I could see Mrs. Campbell laugh.

You did great, she signed.

I thought I'd done all right, but I knew there'd be more to learn tomorrow and the next day and the day after that and the year after that.

Outside, the campus baked silently in the warm September sun. I saw backpacks under trees, and books on picnic tables. Some kids were passing around a football, others a Frisbee. There was a group of four kids kicking a soccer ball back and forth, while some other kids took turns dribbling a basketball. They all seemed to be having fun. Not one of them was wearing a mitt or throwing around a baseball.

I watched a kid leap up and snatch a Frisbee out of the air as it attempted to soar by overhead. Good for him. He could jump and run and throw and not fall down. Wow. How impressed was I? If that had been me, I would've lost my balance and fallen down in front of everyone. But that didn't really matter, because no one had asked me to play, anyway.

The kid who'd caught the Frisbee caught me staring. He raised his eyebrows and waved me into the game. He offered to throw the Frisbee my way.

Though I hadn't needed a cane for a while, and although my balance kept getting better all the time, I didn't want to risk looking like a fool in front of everyone. *No thank you*, I signed. I shook my head and turned away.

I wanted to get back to the dorm. I felt mentally exhausted. Though I didn't think I'd be able to sleep, lying down for a little while sounded great. Plus, the buzzing in my ears had started again. It wasn't loud, but it was annoying, like an itch I couldn't reach to scratch.

Something suddenly knocked me hard from behind. I pitched forward. I thought maybe a ball had hit me in the back. I fell onto the sidewalk, skinning the palms of my hands. When I got up, Eiji, the dark-haired boy from lunch, was standing in front of me.

My hands burned from the injury. I'd never been in any kind of a fight. That incident with Jordan at the baseball field was the closest I'd ever come to it. At least Jordan was my age, and my size. I just stood there with my chest puffed out a little. Eiji mock-laughed and started signing. I had no idea what the creep was saying. Rather than waste my time replying, I turned and walked away.

It had been scary not hearing someone come up behind me. So I suppose I should have expected what would come next, but I didn't. I wasn't prepared when a hand grabbed my shoulder and spun me around. I shrugged the hand off, stepped toward Eiji, and pushed him back a few steps. Frustrated because I couldn't call on the signs I knew to express my feelings, I spoke. "What is your problem, jerk?"

Eiji pointed at his own chest and mouthed the word, *Jerk?*

Could he lip-read? Was he just hard of hearing and not deaf? It didn't matter. I had made things worse. He knew I had called him a jerk. Eiji punched a fist into his palm.

I got the message. He expected a fight and looked like he might actually enjoy hitting people in the face. I didn't want to, but I wasn't about to back down. I crossed my arms, hoping to show that I wasn't easily intimidated, but also hoping to hide my shaking arms.

Samantha appeared as if out of thin air. She pushed her way between us and kept chopping her right hand into the palm of her left. *Stop. Stop. Stop.*

She shot Eiji some pretty fierce-looking hand signs. He signed back.

I realized that anyone who was watching knew what was going on, what was being said. All they had to do was follow the hands of Samantha and Eiji. I was the only one missing out. They signed so fast, I had no idea what was happening.

Maybe things would have been better back at my old school, after all. I was deaf, like everyone around me, but for some reason, I could not consider myself.... what... I wasn't the same as them? Not better than them, but maybe not equal, either.

It was as if the world were spinning at one hundred miles an hour, and I was the only thing on the planet standing still. My knees wobbled. The hissing in my head seemed more insistent. Suddenly, I wanted my cane. I wanted my dorm room. I wanted to be home.

Dr. Stein showed up next. I cringed. He must have asked what was going on because Eiji made a fist near his chin, opened his fingers, spreading his hand wide as it dropped away from his face. *Nothing,* he turned and walked away.

Samantha pointed to my hands. I put them in my pockets. I didn't need a mother on campus. I had one at home.

"I'm alright," I kept saying. "It's okay."

Then she and Dr. Stein signed as if I weren't standing there with them. Samantha nodded and thanked the doctor.

He looked at me. *How are you, Marco?*

I shrugged. My palms burned. I felt embarrassed. Eiji. This was all Eiji's fault. "Fine."

Dr. Stein gave me a look, as if saying, *What do you mean "fine"?* He pointed in the direction Eiji had walked off, establishing Eiji as the subject of our talk, and then he signed: *Trouble?*

I shook my head. "It's nothing."

Want to see the nurse?

"No." I watched the doctor open his black leather day planner. He pulled out a business card, wrote on the backside, and handed it to me. It was an appointment for Friday after lunch. I thought about arguing. I didn't want to talk to him. He seemed all right and everything, but what was there to talk about? Eiji? Was this really such a big deal? It seemed like a waste of time.

I was angry that he'd handed the appointment card to me in front of other kids. Now they'd probably think I was a little crazy. I tucked the card into my back pocket, feeling too drained to know what to say.

Dr. Stein patted me on the back and walked away.

He's a good guy, Samantha signed.

You talk to him?

A lot of us here do. It's nothing to feel weird about.

I don't, I signed, totally lying. *No big deal.*

I did feel funny about it. I wasn't crazy. I wasn't—as Patrick used to say about the guy who walked his dog around the block in pajamas and fireman boots—a few sandwiches short of a picnic. I didn't think I needed to talk with a psychologist.

Want me to show you around? she signed.

I got a tour.

Tours are of the buildings. I bet they didn't show you where we're going. Want to see?

I shrugged. *Sure.*

We walked across campus, toward the back end. The place wasn't all that big. I counted seven buildings. Each building had a large sign with its name on it. We were headed toward the south end of campus, where the boys' and girls' dorms were. The athletic field was behind these buildings, and, as we passed between them, I saw kids playing soccer.

Want to play? Samantha signed.

A kid dribbled the ball down the field, moving fast. Another player came at him and tried to kick the ball away. The boy with the ball juked to the left and right, tricking the other player. Making it look easy, he brought his leg back and kicked the ball toward the goal. The goalie leapt into the air, arms outstretched, but missed the block. The ball glided into the netting. The kid who made the point shot his arms into the air victoriously. It looked like fun.

No, I signed back. *I don't want to play. I'm going back to my room. I have to study.*

Before she could say anything or try to stop me, I turned and walked away.

Chapter 25

At dinnertime, I went to the cafeteria, got in line, and looked around. I didn't want to eat in the packed cafeteria. Everyone seemed to know everyone else. Maybe when I moved into regular classes and didn't spend my days one-on-one with Mrs. Campbell things would be different. Right now, though, the only kid I recognized was Eiji, and I had no intention of sitting at his table. I brought my food back to my dorm room in a Styrofoam container.

After eating, I sat on the bed with my back to the wall and studied a chapter in my sign language book. The lights flicked off and on. I looked up and saw a small boy in the doorway. He smiled, walked into my room, and sat down on the bed across from me.

My name is Kyle, he signed. *I'm eight.*

Kyle, I spelled and nodded. *My name is Marco. I'm twelve.*

He stood up, walked over to me, and we shook hands. Even though he was the same age as Marie, he seemed younger. He was shorter than her, scrawnier. But it seemed like there might be more to it.

Kyle began signing. His hands were all over the place. His fingers looked like he was playing an instrument made out of air. I closed my eyes and shook my head as I held up my hands to stop him. *Slow*, I signed. *You sign too fast.* It amazed me how quickly an eight-year-old could talk with his hands.

Kyle smiled, nodding. *We are roommates.*

For a little kid, Kyle seemed all right. He had dark hair, glasses, and wore two hearing aids. "Can you hear?"

He tilted his head. *Some. Lip-read, too*, he signed. *Can you hear?*

No. I'm deaf.

I thought Kyle would ask a million questions: how long have you been deaf, or, were you born deaf? That kind of thing. Thankfully, he didn't. I still hated answering those questions; it made it all feel too real.

I did notice that deaf people didn't talk in long, complicated sentences. There was shorthand to the language that, little by little, I was picking up. Instead of saying something like, *Do you want to come to the grocery store with me?* A deaf person might just say, *Going to the store. Want to come?*

Just so you know, I sleep with a light on, Kyle signed. *Okay?*

I almost laughed, but didn't. I realized quickly enough that he was serious.

He glanced at my open book. *Good book?*

I held up the textbook so Kyle could see the cover.

Kyle sat on the edge of my bed. He opened his mouth, reached his hand in, and wiggled a tooth. *Loose.*

I nodded, raising my eyebrows and making a face that I hoped would say, *Cool.*

Never lost one here before, he signed. *Scares me.*

Why?

The tooth fairy, Kyle signed. *What if she doesn't know where to find me?*

The fears of an eight-year-old, I thought. *Like Santa,* I signed, *she can find you anywhere.*

You think?

I know, I held the sign to stress my confidence.

He looked relieved, stood up, and went to the door. He stopped, though, and looked at me for a long moment. *You need a sign name.*

You have one? I asked.

Kyle made a letter "K," then brought it across his chest to touch his shoulder.

I repeated the action, trying to commit it to memory. I was being shown so much I didn't think I could retain it all. Not all at once. Not all on the first day.

You always wear one? He pointed at my baseball cap. *The hat?*

I touched the side of my Yankees cap, shrugged and nodded. *Yes.*

Always? Then how about… His face wrinkled as he thought for a second. Then he made the letter "M" and put his hand near his forehead, as if depicting the bill of a ball cap.

I tried it and smiled, nodding in agreement. It felt a little odd, getting a nickname from a boy I'd just met. But in fact, it felt right. I liked my new sign name.

⟡

Shortly after Kyle left and I went back to my studying, the lights flickered on and off again. I looked up, expecting to see Kyle again. Instead, a man stood in the doorway. He waved. I raised my eyebrows at him as if saying, "Just who are you?"

Reading my mind, he signed and spelled, *Hello. My name is Norton. I'm the dorm counselor. I graduated from RSD.*

Ms. Funnel told me each dorm housed a counselor, or DC, on every floor. The DC was an adult who enforced dorm rules, ensured everyone's safety, and handled minor issues, such as disputes between students—a general go-to person for help.

I slid to the corner of my mattress as I introduced myself and invited him into the room. He sat in the chair by my desk.

I was born deaf, he signed. *How about you?* And there came the question I'd been dreading.

I got sick this summer. Meningitis, I spelled. *My fever was so high, I became deaf.*

He nodded, looking at me with a frown. *Sorry. If you need to talk?*

I thought about the cane I was too embarrassed to use. About me limping around campus. I thought about how I walked slowly so I could avoid losing my balance. The last thing I wanted was to fall in front of everyone, or in front of Samantha. *I'm good,* I signed.

Okay. Anytime, you come see me. Norton had brown hair with bangs that draped in front of his face over and well past gold-framed glasses. He wore a plain white T-shirt and baggy jeans. The one thing that stood out was his feet. He had huge feet. His sneakers were so big, they looked cartoonish.

I wasn't sure how to respond, so I signed, *Did you go to college?*

His frown turned into a smile. *I go to Rochester Institute of Technology.*

He gave me a schedule to review. It listed which chores would be mine and the days I'd be responsible for doing them. Next Monday, I'd have to sweep the hallway; Tuesday, take out the trash; Wednesday, dust the lounge area. Nothing too complicated.

Assignments change daily, he signed. The reverse side of the paper showed a calendar with dorm events. Movie night in the lounge, basketball games in the small gym in the basement, story night, and other similar activities. Something was going on every evening. None of it interested me. Not movies—I hated reading subtitles all the time. It took away from the action on the screen. Basketball, yeah, right. If I couldn't swing a bat without falling over, I wasn't going to attempt a lay-up.

If you need something, just ask, Norton reiterated.

After his visit, I went down to the study. No one was on the TTY phone. I decided now would be a good time to call home. I dialed, set the receiver in the computer cradle, and waited for someone to answer. Most kids had cell phones and texted all the time. I thought about asking my parents for one, but I knew money was tight. They'd just spent a fortune installing a machine at home, and rewiring the lights to the phone and the doorbell. At least I wouldn't have to worry about long lines for this phone.

When someone finally answered, I typed: *Hello? It's Marco! GA.* The GA stood for "go ahead," letting whomever I talked to know that I was done typing.

A moment later, a reply appeared across my screen. *Marco! It's Mom. How was the first day of school? GA.*

There were so many ways to answer the question.

I started at the beginning.

Mrs. Campbell is my teacher.

I typed about lunch—pizza, and a bit about not liking Eiji, and about Kyle and Norton.

Dad, Mom and Marie typed up a storm in reply, asking questions about all the people I mentioned. Marie typed: *Whitney's been real good, but I can tell she misses you. But don't worry, I'm taking good care of her. GA.*

I missed Whitney, too. *I know you're taking good care of her. That's why I left you in charge. Give her a dog treat from me, OK? GA.*

A kid was suddenly standing beside me. I hated that about being deaf—not knowing when someone was around me unless I saw them. He stood next to me and pointed to the phone. I wondered if he lived on my floor, but he looked more interested in making a call than introducing himself.

I didn't want to hang up. I looked at the clock on the wall. I'd been on the phone for almost half an hour, longer than I thought. It had to be because of all the time it took to read, type, and transmit messages back and forth. Marie and I typed kind of fast, but that's because we were more used to computers than our parents. *Mom, I've got to go. Someone needs the phone. BYE.*

Lying in bed, I wondered why I had chosen to come to this school. It had been great talking with everyone on the phone, but now they were all home together and I was here, alone.

What in the world was I doing here? Not just at RSD, but why was I even alive? Why did everything have to go so wrong in my life? I couldn't figure out why something like this had to happen to me.

I thought Kyle had been exaggerating when he said he slept with the lights on. I had pictured a Batman nightlight plugged into the outlet closest to his bed. But no, when Kyle said he slept with the light on, he meant THE light. The ceiling fixture seemed to have a three million-watt bulb screwed into it. If I hadn't known better, I'd have sworn the room was drifting on a direct collision course with the sun.

Who knew that sleeping in a dorm full of kids could be so lonely? I used to feel like a big kid at twelve, but right now... I turned to face the wall. I wasn't about to cry or anything. Or maybe I was. My cheeks felt hot and my eyes were moist. I didn't want Kyle to see.

I had never really thought about it before, but having my mom and dad in the bedroom down the hall made all the difference. It made me feel safe.

I concentrated on trying to think about something else, but I'd never felt more lost and alone in my whole life.

CHAPTER 26

O n my second day, Mrs. Campbell promised a challenging session and gave lots of little tests. *You have much to learn*, she explained. Not wanting to discourage me, she added, *You are doing great for how long you have been signing.*

I didn't mind working hard at ASL, especially since everyone else signed so fast I could barely keep up. Like when I played baseball, I didn't just want to be good at throwing the ball, I wanted to be the best pitcher. It was the same with signing: I didn't just want to be good—I wanted to be one of the best. So even after Kyle fell asleep, I stayed up and practiced my signing. Why not? The light was on, anyway.

After that second lesson with Mrs. Campbell, though, I was just exhausted. When classes were over, I simply ran as fast as I could down the halls until I was free. It was refreshing to get outside; I enjoyed the crisp air and smells of autumn. Even with homework ahead of me, the idea of sitting under a tree while doing it sounded way better than feeling trapped inside a classroom, or my dorm room.

It felt good to be outside—until I saw Eiji. The dark-headed bully saw me, too. Though my legs wanted to stop walking, I decided to veer away and look for a tree as far away from him as possible. However, as soon as I changed direction, so did he.

He put his fists on his hips and stepped in front of me on the sidewalk. I don't think I had truly realized before that Eiji was a full two feet taller than me. With his upper lip curled menacingly, he resembled a snarling wolf. His arms were thick—with muscles bigger than any kid that I knew. He must have started working out before he was old enough to walk! He stared at me with eyes that were beady, hard, and cold.

My mouth went dry. I had no idea how to fight, but that didn't stop me from imagining knocking that cocky grin off his face. Instead, I tried to walk casually around him by making a wide arc.

Just as I got past him, I felt a hard push from behind. *Déjà vu.* I should have been ready for the shove, but wasn't. This time, the grass was soft, keeping me from scraping my palms again.

I got back up to my feet and spun around, my stomach in knots. Fighting just wasn't worth it. He was mad at me for a reason. It was my fault mostly. *I am sorry about the other day*, I signed. *Please, leave me alone.* My chest felt tight. I could see kids had turned to look at us. Had this been my old school, the chanting—*Fight! Fight! Fight!*—would already have begun.

Eiji smiled, threw back his head and opened his mouth wide. I knew he was laughing. In my imagination it sounded like the evil cackle of a criminal from some demented low-budget horror movie.

I tried to just walk away. I could feel heat in my cheeks—and wondered just how red they had turned. The kids must have thought I was chicken. Maybe I was.

I prepared for another push in the back. It never came. How could Eiji get away with acting like this? Wasn't he afraid of getting kicked out? I didn't want to get in trouble my first week here.

Ditching the idea about doing homework under a tree, I tried not to run or even hurry as I headed for the dorm. I tried not to look back over my shoulder. Was he following me? Was he about to push me again? Was he still laughing? Was everyone laughing?

My stomach muscles tensed up even more. Messing around with Patrick was the closest I'd ever been to an actual fight. Even though we'd been angry at each other a few times and had come close to throwing punches, something always stopped me. Something had always stopped both of us. It was more than just friendship; it was also me somehow knowing deep down that it wasn't right.

Hitting him wasn't going to solve anything. How many major league ball games had I watched when there'd been bench-clearing fights? Every time, players would get ejected from the game and coaches fined. People even got hurt, and all it did was make me want to turn the television off.

Still, how long could I go on letting Eiji push me around? When I reached the dorm, I turned to glance sideways. Eiji was right where I had left him. He wasn't laughing. But it didn't look like he was breathing, or blinking, or anything, either. He looked like an angry statue. I took the steps two at a time, and once I entered the building, ran down the hall to my room.

Chapter 27

S ince I spent most of my days with Mrs. Campbell, I didn't get much time to meet other kids. So I was pretty stoked when Brian asked me to sit with him at lunch. It would be a good end to my first week.

Some guys and me are going to kick the ball around after lunch, want to play? Brian had signed when I ran into him in the hall that morning. Despite being excited by the invitation, I couldn't help but worry about looking foolish. What would Brian think if he saw how uncoordinated I was? He'd never believe I'd once played baseball, the pitcher for my team, lightning fast around the bases... I was lucky I was getting around without the cane; I couldn't risk anything more in public.

I wish I could, I had signed, relieved at having an excuse. *I meet with Dr. Stein after lunch.* So we had settled on just lunch. Friday marked my first cafeteria meal since the food fight. I felt nervous. I barely ate, and mostly stabbed the food, scraping it from one edge of the plate to the other.

Brian signed, *You don't seem too thrilled about your meeting with Dr. Stein. He's cool. Want me to walk over with you?*

Losing my appetite entirely, I dropped the fork onto the tray and leaned back in the chair. I wished I could have heard the fork clank when it hit, echoing in the almost-empty cafeteria. I didn't know if a lot of people went home early for the weekend or what, but the campus felt deserted.

No, thank you. I'm good. I stood up. *See you on Monday?*

Have a good weekend!

As I wandered out of the cafeteria and over to Dr. Stein's office, I wondered what he might want to talk about—hopefully not the fight with Eiji. That had been so lame. I planned on staying away from Eiji. So it wasn't like there was an issue anymore. As I got closer, I could feel the back of my knees sweating.

I didn't want to be late, but I wasn't in any hurry either. I kept hoping Dr. Stein had been in a rush at the beginning of the week when he wrote out the appointment card and had forgotten to add the date and time to his calendar. At least it was Friday—and I'd be going home for the weekend. Thinking about *that*, I realized I could get through *this*.

Dr. Stein looked up from his desk when I arrived and waved me in. He stood up to shake my hand and then went over and shut the door. The room looked more in order than it had over the summer. And so did the doctor: no more jeans and sneakers. He wore a charcoal-gray suit, with the jacket carefully placed on a hanger on his coat rack. His sleeves were cuffed at the wrist and the knot in his maroon tie was stiffly slotted up against the throat of his white dress shirt. The table that had been in the center of the office was gone. Instead, he now had a leather couch and two recliner chairs. A coffee table occupied the space between them.

How was your first week? he signed.

"Good," I said.

Learning sign language okay?

"Yes," I answered impatiently. I was ready to know what this meeting was about.

I understand you have Mrs. Campbell. How are things going?

"I like her. She's teaching me a lot." I wanted to say more, but instead I looked up at the ceiling. I wasn't sure what each question meant or where it would lead or how he would end up evaluating me because of the things I said or didn't say. I bit down on my lower lip.

What if you answer in sign for this talk? He continued signing. *It helps me keep up on my skills.*

Fine, I signed succinctly.

Want to talk about anything?

Like the fight? It seemed like the whole reason for this visit in the first place. I hadn't wanted to bring it up. It was almost like he tricked me.

If you'd like.

There's nothing to talk about. I gave up on my hands and started to say "Eiji . . ." before cutting myself short. He might be a bully and a jerk, but what more was there to say?

Dr. Stein raised his hands as if agreeing with me. *Did you tell anyone about what happened?*

No. Nothing to tell, really.

I see, he answered. *And how are you adjusting to living here in Rochester?*

It's okay.

And being away from your family?

I'm looking forward to going home for the weekend, I admitted. Dad always tried to make sure everything seemed okay, but I knew he was worried about money. Mom's over-protectiveness drove me a little crazy, but right now, I kind of missed it. I didn't expect my feelings for them to come up so strongly in the doctor's office. I missed them. Even Marie.

I felt tears pool in my eyes. For a moment, my vision blurred. I wiped them away with the back of my hand.

He acted like he didn't notice. *How's everything else?*

I'm doing fine. If anything, it is the static in my ears that is really bothering me, I signed, deciding to change the subject.

That must be bothersome. Is it all the time?

No, I signed. *But it is a lot of the time.*

Is it ringing now?

No.

Dr. Stein shifted his weight around in the chair and signed some more. *I have a different question for you. How has becoming deaf made you feel?*

"Feel? What do you mean?" I was so taken aback by this question that I started speaking again. I was doing fine and didn't need to probe at every nook and cranny in my brain. And I was certainly not going to talk about baseball.

You went from hearing to deaf almost in an instant, he explained. *I am wondering how that change has made you feel. It must be a lot to handle. Anger seems like a natural response. Have you felt angry?*

"Would getting angry give me my hearing back? No," I said. "So why get angry about it? I'm accepting it. There's nothing I can do to change anything that has happened to me. For some reason I must have done something wrong and life is punishing me for it."

He wrote something down on a pad of paper. *Punishment,* he signed. *Do you blame yourself, Marco?*

I don't blame anyone, I signed, but it wasn't true. Someone or something had to be the cause of this. I didn't give myself the disease. I blamed whomever the contagious person was who gave me meningitis. I blamed the doctors for not controlling my fever. I blamed technology for not being able to fix my hearing. I could think of a lot of blame to go around.

But did I blame myself? Good question.

I'd like to meet with you again, Marco.

I guess, I signed.

How about next Friday?

"Sure," I said, standing up. "Why not?"

Have a great weekend and say hello to your family for me.

You, too, I signed, getting out of there as quickly as I could.

CHAPTER 28

D istracted by my appointment with Dr. Stein—I continued to wonder what "was I angry" meant—I absentmindedly made my way back toward the dorm room. The sight of Marie on the lawn made my heart skip a beat. I broke into a sprint and scooped my sister up into my arms. "I missed you," I said. I spun her around.

I missed you, she signed.

"How's Whitney?"

Sign, Marie demanded with her hands.

Fine. How's Whitney?

Fine. Happy. Playful. She misses you, too.

I can't wait to see her. How was your first week of school?

Wonderful! Marie started wriggling with excitement. She hopped from one foot to the other. *I love my teachers and seeing my friends. But I couldn't wait for the first week to be over.*

Why not?

Because I've been waiting for you to come back home, she signed.

I saw Mom and Dad sitting at a picnic table with Patrick. I hugged Marie again and then, holding hands, we ran over to greet everyone else.

Before I could reach Patrick, Mom jumped to her feet and gave me a big hug. She kissed me on the head, cheeks, and lips. I scrunched up my face, squeezing my eyes shut and wrinkling my nose. But inside, I lapped it up— loving every second of it.

When she finally let go, I again tried to greet Patrick, but Dad stepped forward and put out his hand as if it were a fishing pole. I shook it. Then he reeled me in for a big bear hug. I had almost forgotten how strong he was. The air seemed to squirt from my lungs as he nearly crushed me in the embrace. I had missed that about Dad.

All of this—this hugging—made me realize it had been a long first week at school.

I saw Eiji over my father's shoulder. The boy sat on an army duffel bag. I figured it was packed full of dirty laundry. An Asian man in a navy blue suit held a cell phone to his ear as he walked toward Eiji. Cradling the phone against his shoulder, the man pointed at Eiji, barely looking at him, and then waved impatiently for him to come along. As Eiji slowly got to his feet, the man tapped Eiji roughly on the back of the head. Eiji spun around and the man pointed at his watch, as if saying *come on, hurry it up already.*

I let go of my father and watched as he slung the duffel bag over his shoulder and followed a few steps behind. When Eiji glanced over, I was too late in looking away. He'd seen me watching him.

Patrick waved a hand in front of my face. His eyes were open wide, and he was smiling a funny smile. "I didn't forget you." We did our secret shake. "Junior high all right?"

Patrick shrugged, bouncing his head from side to side.

Well? How was the first week here? Dad signed.

Though we had talked every night using the TTY phone, I shrugged. "Kind of okay, I guess."

All packed? Mom signed.

I am.

Let's get your stuff, Patrick signed.

My jaw dropped.

I wanted to surprise you, he signed. *I've been taking sign language classes, too.*

All the things that had happened to me the past several months had been overwhelming. But Patrick learning to sign… they had happened to him, too.

We're friends? Patrick signed.

We're friends! I had to swallow hard. I really didn't want to blubber like a baby there in the parking lot in front of everyone. I knew I would because I could feel my face scrunching up, ready to burst into tears. I could almost see how I would look, and I knew I wouldn't be able to stop. So I did the only thing I could think to do. I punched Patrick in the arm. Patrick hit me back. Then we hugged, slapping each other on the back pretty hard.

I felt a *tap-tap-tap* on my shoulder. I let go of Patrick. Kyle stood behind me with his arms crossed, as if waiting for introductions.

He had a backpack on, and explained he was waiting for his parents to pick him up. My mom and dad were all over him like adoptive parents or something. Marie signed with Kyle, showing off her sign language abilities as Patrick and I walked toward the boys' dorm room.

Patrick worked at engaging me in conversation. His sign language was limited, but he did very well considering he didn't communicate this way all the time. He brought up the weather and asked how school was going. I kept shaking my head, impressed, and savored talking in sign language with my best friend.

In my room, Patrick's expression became more serious. He looked around and picked up a notebook and pen off the dresser. He wrote: *Did you hear about Jessica Ketchum?*

The name sounded familiar. "No? Who is she?"

She was in your sister's class last year. Your family talked about it on the way up here, he wrote.

"What happened?" I asked.

She and her mom were in a car accident. A drunk driver smashed into them, he wrote.

"Are they all right?"

He shook his head. *Jessica's mom died. And Jessica is in the hospital. Your sister is pretty upset about it.*

"She seemed okay," I said.

She was crying, he wrote.

I didn't know what else to say. I grabbed my suitcase and headed down the stairs and out to the parking lot.

I wanted to run right back to where my family was. Things had not gone well for me the last few months. I hated that I couldn't hear, but I was alive. My mom, dad, and little sister were alive. I needed to hug them all over again.

⌒⚬⌒

Patrick, Marie, and I sat in the back on the drive home to Batavia. Mom turned around in the front seat to face everyone. *We'll stop for dinner?*

I rubbed my stomach. Patrick was nodding, and though I couldn't hear my sister, I saw that she was probably spouting off places where she'd like to eat. After all, she'd made the drive more often than I had.

Though I was hungry, I was anxious to get back home. I missed my bedroom, my bed, and everything else about the house. I also wanted to spend some time alone. It was a weird thought, and it might not make sense, but I knew I had not spent enough time feeling sorry for myself. Did I blame myself? I needed time to think about things, but also to unwind, have some time to just play with Patrick—and Whitney! I missed my dog...

No. I definitely wasn't half as hungry as I was homesick.

Chapter 29

I wasn't sure why, but I expected my bedroom to look different. But, there everything was. The posters of baseball players still hung on the walls. The dark blue bedspread was still dark blue. My baseball trophies still sat cluttered on top of the shelf.

Right then, I felt most like my old self. My real self.

I set my iPod on the docking station, turned it on, slowly increased the volume, watched the blue bars move like waves, growing taller and taller, stretching into the red until the volume was up as loud as it could go and the display showed nothing but a red, digital block. The Smithereens. I knew the song that was playing, but I couldn't hear it. I couldn't hear a thing, but I did feel *something*. The vibration from the music was coming through the floorboards, tickling the soles of my feet. The booming of the bass guitar and pounding of the bass drum pushed its way up from the floor, stimulating the carpet and igniting my feet. And the tempo was there. I felt it.

My legs began moving to the rhythm My body sensed the vibrations. I started to rock from side to side. I bobbed my head and twisted down toward the ground before coming back up again.

I felt the music. I could not hear the singing, but… I felt the music!

Spinning around to the beat, I caught Mom, Dad, and Marie standing in the doorway, holding their hands over their ears. I continued to dance, not missing a beat and smiling. "I can feel it!" I yelled. "I can feel the music!"

Mom clapped her hands together. She walked into the room and started dancing, too. She reached out her hands and caught hold of mine. She pulled me in, hugging me tight. Her hot tears wet my neck. When she let go, she was smiling. And we danced some more.

Dad didn't wait long. He bowed before Marie. Marie did a curtsey. With the formalities out of the way, they jumped around dancing to the fast and heavy beat.

6✇9

Saturday morning, the lights in the kitchen flickered. I went to see who was ringing the doorbell. Patrick stood on the front step wearing his leather mitt and cradling a baseball in it. He raised his eyebrows, silently asking if I wanted to play.

I did. I longed to play. Though my balance was a lot better, I knew I'd never be able to throw the way I used to, or catch, or hit, or run... Even if I didn't fall down or embarrass myself, the truth would always be right there in front of me, staring me in the face. I could never be the player I was before I became sick. Never. "Nah. No, thank you."

Patrick took off the mitt and tucked it with the ball under his arm so he could sign. *Why not?*

"I just don't feel like it," I answered.

He pretended to ride a bicycle, and then raised his eyebrows again.

I shook my head. "Nah." The bike was in the garage where it belonged. It had been terrifying during the summer when we'd ridden to the ballpark. I hadn't tried riding it since. The last thing I needed was to have a car hit me and be laid up with broken bones for the next few months—or worse. "Want to come in?"

He shrugged. It was a sunny morning. We never spent sunny days inside. Or, we never used to. "We could play video games," I offered. I had slipped in the baseball game last night after dancing with my family and was surprised to find that I really enjoyed it. I might not be able to hear the sound effects, but it was still fun to play.

Okay, he signed.

We set up in the living room and played for about an hour. Patrick wanted to be the Mets. I, of course, had first dibs on the Yankees. We played seven innings. We took turns being up to bat, on defense, in the field. The game involved a lot of fast finger action, hitting one button on the controller to have a man steal a base, selecting the right pitch to confuse the player up to bat. Patrick and I played the same way. We couldn't sit still and just work the controller. We had to twist our bodies this way and that, as if our doing so made the electronic players respond more favorably. Unfortunately, the Mets won, 10 to 7.

"Play again?" I was ready to hit the reset button.

Patrick made up an excuse about needing to head home to help his mother with something. But I saw the way he picked up his mitt and ball on the way out. He was headed to the ballpark. On a day like today, there'd be a game going on. He would want in. I couldn't blame him. A part of me wanted in, too.

CHAPTER 30

Entering the cafeteria at lunchtime on Monday was different from being home over the weekend and going into my own kitchen for lunch, that's for sure. I was already homesick.

Kyle sat alone at a table, working in a notebook with his math book open in front of him.

Homework? I signed, after setting my tray down next him.

He nodded.

Have a good weekend? I signed.

Slow. I don't have any brothers or sisters. There aren't many kids to play with on my street. I like it better here, he signed. *You?*

Great weekend, I admitted. I didn't want to tell him I was already looking forward to the next one.

He picked up his hamburger with relish, took a big bite, and winced.

Okay? I signed.

My tooth, he signed and reached his fingers into his burger-filled mouth. Somehow in all of that mess he managed to find and pull out his tooth. Smiling, he went on chewing his food, holding his tooth in the air and admiring it like a trophy.

I saw Samantha and her friend, Brian, step out of the cafeteria line and glance around for a place to sit. I raised my arm and waved them over.

Hi, guys, she signed.

Brian gently thrust his chin out in greeting, before they both set their trays down.

Kyle lost his tooth, I signed.

Samantha clasped her hands together. She looked so excited about the news, which was funny, because now Kyle didn't seem to be interested anymore. He stood up, wrapped his tooth in a napkin and tucked it into his pants pocket. Sitting down, he went back to his meal as though nothing significant had just happened.

Samantha looked questioningly at me. I just raised my eyebrows and shrugged. Turning so Kyle wouldn't see, I signed, *I think he's afraid the tooth fairy will not know where he is*, and then winked.

You know what? Brian signed to Kyle, *I lost some of my teeth here, and some at home, and the tooth fairy found me, no matter where I was!*

Kyle didn't look relieved.

How is geography class going? I asked, changing the subject.

Brian shrugged. *Not my favorite so far.*

Not mine, either, agreed Samantha.

He smiled a big smile. *I'll be happy to get any grade that is passing.*

What are you guys doing tonight? Samantha signed.

Why? Brian signed.

They're showing a movie tonight in the theater. That new one, the comedy about that guy who wakes up and is somehow turned into a nine-year-old kid, she explained.

I have wanted to see that one since it came out in the summer, Brian signed. *I hate that we have to wait so long for a version with subtitles to be released before we can go see a movie. I'm in. What about you, Marco?*

I had seen it last spring. Even Batavia's tiny theater got movies quickly in comparison to the deaf community. How funny could it be with subtitles? *Sure. Why not?*

It starts at seven. We can meet for dinner and then head over? she signed.

Sure. Brian and I signed.

What about you, Kyle? I tried to include my roommate.

I'll pass. I got chess club tonight, he signed. I noticed his tongue kept licking at the gum where his tooth had been attached moments ago.

CHAPTER 31

I sat in the small lounge in the dormitory using the TTY to talk with Patrick who was at my house using my family's machine. *We're all going to see a movie after dinner,* I typed. My stomach growled. It was almost time to eat. *We are seeing that comedy with the guy who wakes up and he's a kid, GA.*

We saw that together, remember? Good movie. The rest of Patrick's response scrolled across the screen. *How u going 2 C the movie? Does someone interpret? GA.*

No. The movie has subtitles. GA.

Patrick wrote back: *OIC. How's this Brian kid? GA.*

Pretty cool. He plays soccer and stuff, GA.

Patrick replied: *Soccer's cool. You play soccer there? GA.*

Even though I knew Patrick wouldn't believe me—or wouldn't understand, I typed: *Not me. I'm not into sports. Look, it is almost dinnertime. I got to go, SK,* I typed, telling Patrick I was about to hang up. *CUL,* I typed for "see you later."

It had been pretty cool out earlier and the sky looked dark now, so I decided to go back to my room for a coat. Fall was such a drastic change from summer. One day it could be 90 degrees, the next 60. Rochester was funny that way. Someone had once said, "If you don't like the weather here, wait five minutes. It'll change." I thought it had been a joke. Who'd have guessed the guy was serious?

I grabbed my coat and left my room, thinking that going to a movie with my new friends would be exactly what I needed to help feel better about being away from home.

Eiji stood in the hall, halfway between my room and the stairs. The way he stood, grinning, made me know he was here for me.

Watch it, I signed.

Where are you off to? Eiji signed.

I slung my coat over my shoulder and tried walking by him without answering. He used his shoulder to knock me back a few steps.

I asked you a question.

I could not figure out why this kid had it in for me. I didn't want trouble. I didn't want to fight. All I wanted was for him to leave me alone. *Can't we forget about the other day and just start over?* I signed.

He shook his head and signed, *No*.

Too bad. I put out an arm to try to push my way past. I didn't want to keep Brian and Samantha waiting.

Eiji was like a tree. He didn't budge. *Too bad for you*, he signed. *Worried about keeping your date with Samantha?* Eiji mocked Samantha's sign name, wiggling his butt as he wiggled his wrist near the corner of his mouth.

Stop it. I guessed Eiji must have seen me with Samantha and Brian at lunch. He probably watched us signing and knew about our plans.

He shook his head and pulled open the door to the broom closet.

I knew by the look on Eiji's face what he had in mind. I turned to run back to my room. I did not want him to catch me. My mind raced. My heart beat fast and hard inside my chest, and it built up like pulsing pressure inside my skull. I breathed quick, shallow breaths. I was afraid.

Hands grabbed me from behind. I lost my footing and fell. Eiji flung himself on top of me. He was not just bigger than me, he was heavier, too. I screamed for help. I was screaming so loud—I just knew that I was. My neck muscles strained, and my jaw hurt from opening my mouth that wide. No one could hear me. I couldn't even hear me.

Eiji got to his feet and lifted me to mine. He grabbed my arms and muscled me into the closet. He gave me a big push with his foot and closed the door.

I tried the knob. The door wouldn't open. I thought that maybe the door wasn't locked, that he might just be on the other side holding it shut. I threw my shoulder against the wood. Nothing happened. The way my shoulder ached, I guessed it was locked. I pounded my fists and screamed for help. Then I had to laugh. Who was going to hear me? Kyle would be at Westervelt

Hall until seven for his chess lessons. He was the only chance I had because he was the only person on the floor who wore a hearing aid.

The tiny room was dark. Only a beam of light came in from under the door.

I couldn't just stand there. I had to try getting out somehow. "Let me out of here," I screamed, beating my fists on the door. "Someone? Somebody? Help me!"

After a while I sat on the floor and leaned back against a box of what smelled like cleaning detergent. Time passed agonizingly slow. Periodically, I kicked at the door, calling out for help. I had no idea if anyone would be able to hear the commotion I made. I figured I needed to keep making noise, or I might not get out of the closet until someone needed a broom or something. But making noise was the way hearing people think. I wasn't a hearing person any longer, and I lived with people who couldn't hear. That gave me an idea.

I opened a bottle of cleaning detergent and poured the whole bottle out into the hall from the space under the door. Someone would have to see the mess. I felt around in the darkness and found some rags. I started to slide them out under the door as well. Maybe Norton, the dorm counselor, would pass by and see the mess.

While killing time, I worked my hands through the alphabet in sign language, first having both hands make the letters from A to Z, then by letting the letters alternate from hand to hand. I must have dozed off and had no idea how long I'd been asleep. All I knew for sure was that I had to have missed the movie. What woke me was the strong smell of the cleaning detergent. It burned my nose when I breathed and made my eyes tear. I'd have to force the door open one way or another. I stood up and put both hands on the knob, and was about to throw my shoulder into the door again when the knob turned easily. The door opened. At some point, someone—*like Eiji*—must have unlocked it.

Relief flooded through me but quickly turned to anger. I strode down to see if Norton was in his room. I wanted to tell him Eiji attacked me and that Eiji threw me into the broom closet and that Eiji locked me in there and that Eiji has been nothing but big fat trouble for me since I got there! Norton's door was open. He sat at a small study desk, absorbed in a book. I found the light switch on the wall and flipped it on and off to get his attention.

He looked up from his reading and smiled.

Suddenly, I was at a loss for words. Now was my chance. I wanted to tell Norton that Eiji was dangerous and that someone should call his parents to come and drag him out of school. Then I pictured Eiji's father in his suit, on his phone, slapping Eiji on the back of the head. Maybe Eiji deserved to get into trouble, but what would telling Norton accomplish? There had to be another way.

Everything all right, Marco? Norton used my sign name.

I was at a loss for words. I forced myself to smile. *Just saying goodnight.*

Goodnight, Norton signed, and went back to his book. He didn't push me to talk. If he had, I might have told him about what happened.

I walked toward my room, stopping to clean up the detergent. I used the rags to wipe up the mess. I closed the broom closet door. *Eiji.* I knew I would have to find a way other than telling on him to change things between Eiji and me.

When I reached my room I saw Kyle was asleep. The clock on the night-stand said it was 9:20 p.m. I took a deep breath and went over to the window. Outside it was raining, but it didn't matter. I wasn't going anywhere now. I wanted to explain to Samantha and Brian what had happened, but it was too late. The movie would be over and Brian was probably in his room. I hoped they weren't mad, thinking I had ditched them.

I slipped off my clothes and into a pair of pajamas.

Before I got into bed, I remembered something. I went to my dresser and took out some money. Quietly as I could, I went over to Kyle's bed. Then I had to smile to myself. His hearing aid was on the nightstand. I could make all the noise I wanted. I didn't need to creep around the room.

But lifting his pillow might.

Very gently, I slipped my hand under his pillow and felt what I was looking for—a little wad of paper napkin with a small, hard tooth in it. I swapped it for the money.

Rather than throwing the tooth away, I went to the bathroom and flushed the tiny package down the toilet before going to bed. I didn't want to be responsible for Kyle finding out that the tooth fairy couldn't find him here at RSD.

CHAPTER 32

Though it had taken time, I gradually became used to the vibrating bed that served as my alarm clock. However, this morning, it was Kyle who shook me awake.

I looked at my roommate who was waving money around and smiling as if he was leading a parade. *What?*

The tooth fairy. He bounced up and down. *I didn't think she'd know how to find me!*

I told you not to worry. I took the money from him and studied it, trying to make my expression match his. I opened my eyes and my mouth wide. Using exaggerated hand motions to illustrate my excitement I signed, *I knew she'd find you!*

As I came out of my dorm I saw Samantha coming out of hers. I was on my way to the cafeteria for breakfast, and assumed Samantha was, too. I knew she'd seen me and could tell by the exaggerated way in which she passed Forrester Hall that I was in trouble. I ran to catch up and tapped her on the shoulder. She didn't stop walking. I went out a few steps in front of her and started walking backwards.

Aren't you going to breakfast? I signed.

Why didn't you show for dinner last night? she responded. She made sort of a grunting face at me and turned around, heading toward Westervelt Hall, even though classes didn't start for another hour.

I caught up to her—and again—walked backwards in front of her. *I can explain.*

She shrugged, as if she did not care. *So you missed the movie. No big deal. But you could have let Brian or me know. We waited around for you and were almost late going in.*

Eiji, I signed.

She stopped and gave me a startled look, like, *oh yeah?*

He locked me in the broom closet last night. I was trapped until nine, I signed.

Samantha's face softened. *For real?*

For real.

Why didn't you text?

I don't have a phone... yet, I signed. *When you gave me your number, I wrote it down, but . . .*

I'm sorry I didn't give you a chance to explain, she signed. *That makes me mad. Eiji. He's bad news. I should have known something was up when you didn't show. But more than that, I should have known Eiji was somehow behind it. I just never thought he'd do something serious like this!*

No problem. What about Brian? Is he mad? I signed.

He wasn't happy. But when you tell him what happened, he'll understand. So, what did *happen?*

I was on my way when Eiji became a real jerk. He pushed me into the closet and locked it.

What did Norton do when he found out? she asked.

I shook my head. *I didn't tell Norton—I'm not telling anyone, only you and Brian.*

Why not? He deserves to get into trouble, she signed.

I didn't want to discuss it. Not anymore. I signed, *So I missed a good movie?*

She shook her head as if she knew I was merely changing the subject. *It was all right,* she signed.

That's it? I smiled. *It was all right?*

She smiled. *Actually, it was awesome. You going to eat breakfast?*

No doubt.

Come on, I'll tell you about it.

We turned around and headed back for the cafeteria.

It starts with this guy getting in his car, and when he starts it, the thing explodes! Samantha's hands came alive with the retelling.

I love explosions!

You'd have loved this one, then. I could almost feel the heat from the flames coming off the screen, she assured me. *If they show it again, I guess I wouldn't mind seeing it a second time if you still wanted to go.*

That sounds cool, I signed. I'd seen it, but she was so excited I didn't want to risk ruining the moment.

⁊⥒⦾

Mrs. Campbell smiled when I entered the classroom. *How are you?* She signed.

I am well, I signed. If I didn't tell Norton about the stunt Eiji pulled, I sure wasn't going to tell a teacher. *And you?*

Fine, thank you. This afternoon, you and I are going to start attending all your regular classes. How does that sound?

I wasn't sure how that sounded. I had enjoyed meeting one-on-one with Mrs. Campbell. I knew I'd learned a lot, and quickly. She was one of the best teachers I'd ever had. It wasn't just because she had patience, though that helped. It wasn't just because she was stern, either, though that helped, too.

What's wrong, Marco?

She made me feel like she actually liked me. I knew working my way into the classrooms meant that sooner or later I'd have to give up Mrs. Campbell.

I don't want to lose you for a teacher, I answered.

Her cheeks turned red. *I can only teach you sign language. The other teachers at this school will teach you everything else you need to learn. They'll teach you all the things other twelve-year-old junior high school students are learning. You don't want to fall behind, do you?*

No. I don't want to fall behind. I was always a pretty good student before… not all "A"s or anything, but I did all right.

But you're scared to move forward? she signed.

I hadn't really thought about it that way, but I guessed it was true. *A little.*

That's normal. Don't be worried. I'm not going to just drop you out of the nest. We'll take things one day at a time. And you know what else? I'm not going anywhere. If you need me, you know where to find me.

All I could picture was me sitting at a desk staring blankly at some teacher signing so fast that all I could see was the blur of her hands waving around in front of her. Then, as I looked side to side, the other kids nodding in agreement with whatever in the world it was the teacher signed. At last, only to find them all turned, staring at me, waiting for me to answer some question I didn't even see signed. What a nightmare!

Mrs. Campbell stood up.

What? I signed. *We're going now?*

She nodded, smiling. *It'll be okay. You'll see.*

She led me to my first real class at RSD. I felt like a puppy being taken on a walk. I stayed a few steps behind Mrs. Campbell as we went down the hall. I watched as she entered the room with a wave of encouragement for me to follow.

The teacher sat behind a desk at the front of the room. She was a big round woman with short black hair and a big smile that only got bigger when she saw me enter. Eight students had their desks arranged in a "U" shape around where the teacher sat. I guess this way everyone could see everyone else in the class. Three girls. Five boys. And just my luck—Eiji was one of them. Then the teacher pointed me to an empty seat directly across from him.

The teacher stood up. *My name is Mrs. Stokes. Everyone, this is Marco Lippa. He will be joining our class, and Mrs. Campbell will be sitting in with him for this week. Marco is new to RSD. Let's all make him feel welcome.*

Everyone greeted me with a *hello* or *what's up.* I waved. I'd seen many of the kids around campus. I sat down beside Mrs. Campbell and waited for the teacher to resume.

Do you have a sign name? Mrs. Stokes asked.

I nodded, and did the letter M near my head, like a baseball cap.

She repeated it. Out of the corner of my eye, I could see Eiji mock me—making his hand like a talking puppet in front of his forehead. I turned my attention quickly to the teacher. She hadn't missed a thing. She rolled her eyes.

That's enough, Eiji, Mrs. Stokes signed. I figured having him in her class meant she knew all about Eiji's personality quirks.

I saw some of the kids laugh. I was thankful I couldn't hear the sound of the laughter.

This is literature, Marco, explained the teacher, *and I was just saying to the class that, at the end of the week you'll be given a copy of* The Outsiders, *by S.E. Hinton to read for an assignment. Has anyone ever heard of it or read it?*

Everyone answered no, or shook their heads. I raised my hand.

Marco? You've heard of it?

I think it was a movie?

That's right. But the book is a bit different than the movie, she signed. *I promise that when we take the test after you have all read the book, there will be plenty of questions based on the book that were not part of the movie. But don't worry. You'll love the book. It is an exciting novel about teen gangs, and family, and loyalty.*

What she didn't know was that although I might end up enjoying the book—there was no way I could ever imagine enjoying the class. Not with Eiji sitting directly across from me. As she taught about plot, setting, and climax, he simply glared at me.

I did catch other students sneaking looks at me, too. And I guess they caught me looking at them. Unlike Eiji, however, no one seemed mean or angry. Just curious about me. I know I was curious about them.

Mrs. Campbell kept patting me on the back in a reassuring way, but it only made me feel like a special case. I wanted out. I wanted to go back to our little one-on-one classroom.

After class, I tried to rush out of the room and be anywhere but there. Mrs. Campbell asked me to wait, then she went over and started signing with the teacher.

Trying not to watch as Eiji gathered up his books, I decided to wait in the hall.

When Eiji came out of the classroom he bumped me with his shoulder as he passed by.

"Jerk," I mumbled.

He turned around and stared at me. Had he heard what I said?

He shook his head, *Why didn't you tell anyone when I locked you in the closet?*

I just shrugged. I didn't have a real answer. I had wanted to tell. Maybe I was just chicken?

Loser. He opened his mouth and laughed a silent laugh, then walked away.

CHAPTER 33

B rian stood by the edge of the gorge and threw stones down into the raging river, while Samantha sat on a rock, her arms behind her, hands planted on the face of the boulder for support. She kept her head tilted back and let the sun shine on her face. I stood between them, hands in my pockets, and just took it all in. This is where Samantha had planned on taking me when she wanted to give me her own special tour of the grounds, but I hadn't let her get past the soccer field.

The sky looked bluer than I'd ever noticed. Not a cloud in sight. Birds flew from tree to tree, but never seemed to leave the area. Perhaps they were enjoying the day, too.

The air smelled fresh and clean. It seemed like we were deep in the woods, like maybe out in the Adirondack Mountains, instead of on a school campus surrounded by the city of Rochester. It seemed like the wooded area stretched on for miles, instead of just into someone's backyard on the other side of the trees. The reality of where we were, in the city, didn't stop me from excitedly pretending we were deep in the wilderness.

Brian turned his back on the river and sat on a rock across from Samantha. *I told my dad I wanted to be a doctor when I grow up,* Brian signed.

I almost laughed. *You're going to be a doctor?*

Sure. Why not?

I'm not sure anyone has told you, but you're deaf, I signed.

He looked at me like I might be crazy. He stood, leaned over, and tapped Samantha on the shoulder. She opened her eyes, raising an eyebrow.

Marco thinks I can't be a doctor when I get older, he signed with agitated movements.

Samantha sat up straight, rigid. *Why not?*

He's deaf, I reminded her.

So?

So? So when a patient comes to him and complains about what hurts and what is wrong, are they going to have to write it all down, or are all of his patients going to have to learn ASL?

Ever hear of Dr. Angela Earhart? She works right here in Rochester at Strong Memorial Hospital. She's deaf, Brian signed.

How does she talk with sick people? I had to ask.

An interpreter assists with phone calls, and in person, Brian signed.

What about you? Samantha asked me, after an awkward moment without any signing.

Me? I always wanted to be a baseball player. The words came rushing out before I remembered I had been hiding that part of myself from them.

But not anymore? Brian asked.

I shook my head. *Not anymore.*

Why not? Samantha asked.

I was about to answer with, "because I am deaf," but held back. *There are no all-deaf teams,* I signed.

Why do you have to play on an all-deaf team? Brian signed.

There is more to life than baseball, I signed. Changing the subject, I turned to Samantha. *What about you?*

She smiled, her hands quickly answering. *I am going to be a critically acclaimed artist.*

For a few moments we signed back and forth talking about her artwork. I wasn't completely paying attention. Brian knew what he wanted to be, and so did Samantha. I tried to be happy for them. It wasn't easy. The envy I felt was a little overwhelming.

Do you believe in God? Samantha signed.

God? I shrugged and nodded.

Do you pray?

If she didn't look so serious, I'd have laughed. *No.*

You believe in God, but you don't talk with Him?

What would we talk about?

She offered up a thin smile. *He likes to hear what's going on.*

Doesn't He just know what's going on?

She nodded. *But He likes to hear from you.*

I squirmed. *You pray?*

All the time.

What do you talk to Him about? I signed.

Sometimes, I talk to Him about you. I ask for Him to give me strength and courage. When we talk, I don't feel so all alone.

And He answers you?

She grinned. *Not so I can hear Him, silly. But He's listening. And in a way, He does answer.*

How?

I asked Him to let me make a good friend. And then you showed up.

Now it was my turn to smile.

CHAPTER 34

The extreme hollow feeling inside my chest ached. Every morning, I wandered the halls during a class break, passing by Dr. Stein's door once or twice—three times, really. Even though I knew I didn't *need* to talk to a doctor, I kind of liked Dr. Stein. He made it easy enough to talk.

Anyway, I knew the doctor was a busy man, probably caught up in a bunch of meetings all day long. Still, all week I had found myself peering into his office, hoping he would have a minute for me. Then I would hurry to class and forget I'd even gone that way looking for him in the first place. I guess I'd have to wait to discuss this feeling with him at our appointment. I figured that if anyone could understand why I felt hollow, it would be him.

When I snuck a look into the office right before the scheduled time, I was surprised to see Dr. Stein typing furiously on his computer keyboard. Too caught up in his work to notice me. Too caught up to care.

We had booked this appointment a week ago, but if he forgot about it, then no big deal. I had other things to do, like get ready to head home for the weekend.

I turned around decidedly. I had tried. What more could anyone want from me? Going over to Dr. Stein's had been a mistake, and a foolish one at that.

My muscles tensed when I felt someone tap me on the shoulder. Turning around, I saw Dr. Stein, a pencil spinning between the fingers of his hands. And he was smiling. *Marco! Right on time,* he signed.

I shrugged. "If you're busy… " Part of me suddenly hoped we could reschedule, or just forget the whole thing. "You looked pretty busy. I don't want to disturb you while you're working."

I was just working until you got here. Now that you are here, let's talk.

He closed the door behind us as we entered his office. Just like last time, everything looked neat and orderly. Sunlight shone in through the window like a spotlight on the chairs we sat in.

"What do we talk about this time?" I asked. *I'm sorry*, I signed, *I forgot you like to have these sessions in sign language.*

Your sign language is really coming along, he signed, nodding like he was impressed.

I smiled, nodding back. *I guess.*

We stared at each other for a moment. I broke eye contact and looked at the floor, up at the ceiling, and then around the room.

Dr. Stein waved to get my attention. *How are things with Eiji?*

We're in English literature together, I signed. *As soon as class ends, I take off to my next class.*

No more trouble?

I shrugged. *I don't hang around long enough for trouble to start. His dorm room, I found out, was on the floor above mine. When I see him coming, I go somewhere else.*

Is that fixing the problem, or avoiding it? Have you thought about talking with him?

"I'm not afraid of anybody, but have you seen the size of him?" I said. "Besides, I think we resolved things between us."

His eyebrows arched.

I'd said too much.

Yeah? How? He signed. *He let it go?*

I threw a french fry at him. He locked me in a closet. We were even. "Without fighting."

Well, good. I'm relieved to hear that, he signed. *Can I ask you a personal question?*

I guess, sure.

How did you become deaf?

The bluntness of the question caught me off guard. *I got real sick*, I signed, spelling "meningitis." *I guess I almost died. When I woke up in the hospital, I couldn't hear.*

How did that make you feel?

I never thought about it, why? I asked. *People born deaf have never had the benefit of hearing sounds before. They might not understand what it is they are missing.*

And you?

I tried to smile, but couldn't.

His question was raw, tough—not a question that could be answered with a simple "yes" or "no."

I had once been able to hear rivers running, birds singing, and car horns honking. I would, perhaps, never hear them again, but at least I'd *heard* them.

Was it better that I had once known sounds, or worse?

I only knew one thing for certain: the sounds of silence were deafening.

I don't know how I feel.

I looked away from the doctor, casting my gaze to the floor. I studied the laces on my sneakers for a moment, then the design on the carpeting. I thought about what Samantha and I had talked about—God. For the first time I wondered why God had let this bad thing happen to me.

Had I done something wrong?

Was my being deaf some kind of punishment from Him?

I closed my eyes and tried to remember what it was I'd done so wrong that God felt the need to steal my hearing away.

Dr. Stein tapped me on the shoulder to get my attention. *There is nothing wrong with feeling one way or the other.*

In a way I feel like I can't do anything anymore, I admitted.

What do you mean? Is there something you are having trouble with?

During the summer I had trouble walking, riding my bike, and playing catch with a ball, but I didn't say anything. I stayed quiet.

What do you want to be when you grow up? Dr. Stein signed.

What did I want to be, or what do I want to be now? I was confused.

Interesting. Are they different now—the things you want and wanted to be?

"Different? Yeah. I guess they are."

So what did you want to be before you became deaf?

I took off my ball cap. "A major league ballplayer," I said. "Now that I'm deaf, that can never happen."

He sat back in his chair for a moment, crossed his legs. He let his right hand caress his chin as if stroking the hairs of an invisible goatee. *There are a lot of famous people in the world who are deaf, Marco*, he signed. *Athletes, too.*

I'm sure there are. I went back to signing in an attempt to appear calmer.

Dreams don't have to end just because you can't hear. Sometimes you need to realign your dreams, but dreams don't have to end.

All I've ever wanted is baseball.

Then I say don't give up on that dream, he signed.

Easier said than done, I thought. I decided to tell Dr. Stein about what happened during the summer when I played ball with kids I thought were my friends.

It's unfortunate that that happened, Dr. Stein signed. *But as you know, people can be cruel. You can't let other people stand in your way if you're chasing after a dream. And some dreams, Marco, are tougher to obtain, whether a person can hear or not.*

I knew what Dr. Stein meant.

My dad had given me the same talk once, explaining how when he was a kid, he planned to grow up and become a rock star. Not everyone grew up to be famous just because they once dreamed of one day doing so.

"It's not just because Jordan was a jerk, it's more than that. I wanted to go out there and play ball like everything was still exactly the same—like nothing had changed." I wasn't calm. My throat burned. I could feel my face getting hot. The tears brimmed on my eyelids, clouding my vision. I swiped at them with my forearm.

Things had changed, though, hadn't they?

"I just love baseball so much. I love being out on the field, and up to bat, and on the pitcher's mound. I love to look over and see my family in the bleachers. There is nothing I loved more than playing baseball. At least back then, but now… swinging a bat, throwing a ball—I can't keep my balance. Deaf athletes who have buzzing inside their head and lose their balance when they throw a ball don't make it to the majors," I said. "I'll never play for the Yankees now."

He nodded. I could tell the wheels were turning in his brain the way he furrowed his brow and pressed his lips together. *Becoming a major league ballplayer is a challenge for hearing people*, he signed.

Tell me about it, I signed.

I imagine the challenge is even harder for a deaf person, he added.

Don't rub it in, I thought.

But if you give up on your dream, you will never know what could have been, he concluded.

CHAPTER 35

THANKSGIVING BREAK

C lasses let out at the usual hour on Wednesday, though everyone thought the teachers would let us leave early for the four-day holiday weekend. After gathering my things, I raced from my room, down the hall toward the stairs, anxious to see Mom and Dad.

Outside, brutally cold air struck me. Shrugging my shoulders and tightening my muscles did little to make me warm.

We were still a month away from winter. But the temperatures had stayed in the forties and fifties since the end of October.

A few times when it rained, it looked like some snow was mixed in there. None of the snow—if you could call it that—stayed on the ground. I watched my breath puff out in clouds as I stood searching the area for my family. Parents were almost running across campus, trying to find their kids. Everyone rushed to and from the buildings.

The campus was always covered with people walking around or out playing—especially around meal times. And Fridays always made things a little more hectic. But this Wednesday was unreal. Forget hectic. People looked frantic. Must've been everyone was excited about getting home and enjoying the holiday break.

I set down the suitcase. My fingers felt numb, so I pulled on my gloves while I waited.

Samantha had gone home at lunchtime after introducing Kyle and me to her father. Her parents were divorced. She had not mentioned that before this week. She explained that her mother and father split the holidays up. This year Thanksgiving was with her father. She would spend Christmas with her mother.

I thought about this while waiting for my parents. On top of being deaf, Samantha had to deal with a divorce. Patrick's parents were divorced, and he hated it. It confused him. He never knew what weekend was with whom. Making plans was always a nightmare. Like Samantha, though, Patrick did not talk much about it.

I couldn't imagine what it would be like if my parents ever decided to separate. Just the thought of it was awful. What if they asked me to choose who I wanted to live with? I would hate to have to answer that one.

Standing by the tall maple tree between my dorm and the parking lot, I saw Eiji slip that worn army duffel bag off his shoulder. He blew into his cupped hands and rubbed his palms together. He wore only a thin fall coat that didn't look like it could do much to battle the chilling wind that whipped around us.

It made no sense at all, but I decided to walk over to Eiji. *Excited about Thanksgiving?* I signed. We hadn't talked since he locked me in the broom closet, and except for that short exchange about me not telling on him, he hadn't been in my face since then, either.

Get lost, he signed.

At least I tried, I thought, ready to walk toward the parking lot. Instead, I took one more shot at it. *What is your problem?*

You don't give up, do you? You haven't figured it out?

No.

I can't make this any simpler, Eiji signed, looking past me, distractedly. *My problem is you.*

I could tell I wasn't the center of Eiji's attention. I turned to see the competition. This time the man in the expensive suit wore a long, dark trench coat and leather driving gloves. Again, he was talking animatedly, but this time with a Bluetooth in his ear, one finger pointed to it as if it were an antenna for better reception. Eiji's father.

Stepping away, I watched as Eiji asked his father to carry the duffel bag. He explained that his hands were cold. The father, never breaking away from the phone conversation, stood stiff with one hand planted on his hip, then pointed at the bag and pointed at Eiji. It wasn't sign language, but the jerky and angry hand motions made his point. Eiji picked up the bag and slung it over his shoulder.

When Eiji looked over at me, he didn't resemble the monster, the bully I'd come to know. The anger was gone, replaced only by a desperate look of silent shame... or was it of nothingness?

CHAPTER 36

I could smell the turkey roasting in the oven when I woke up Thursday morning. I purposely hadn't set my alarm clock. I wanted to sleep in—I looked forward to it. Getting up every morning for school drained me. Besides, everyone knew preteens were teenagers in training, really. We needed to sleep past noon on vacations and weekends, or else we would never be prepared for teenhood.

After taking a long, hot shower and getting dressed, I went downstairs. I wasn't prepared to see both sets of grandparents. They were all sitting around the table. Papa Phil and Grandma Patty sat across from each other, and at opposite ends sat Papa Ray and Grandma Joanne.

Papa Phil and Grandma Patty were Dad's parents. They moved to Tucson, Arizona two years ago after Papa Phil retired. I knew my parents talked about visiting out West during Christmas break, if not this year, then next. What would Christmas be like without snow? I couldn't imagine it, but a trip across the country—that'd be an awesome adventure. I'd been desperate to see the Grand Canyon with my own two eyes ever since I saw pictures of it in a book when I was eight.

Papa Ray and Grandma Joanne were Mom's parents. They lived in Vermont now. When they used to live here, they had a supercool house with a jungle gym in the backyard. They came to all my baseball games. I missed them, so it was great having them home.

I had no idea anyone would be joining us for the holiday. My eyes got wide and my hands flew up in the air. Excitedly, I said, "Hello!"

Look who's here, Marie signed.

My smile wilted. My grandparents didn't normally come to Batavia for Thanksgiving. I knew why they were here. It was because of me. I was worried about what this meant.

Grandma Patty came at me. She hugged me with the strength of a bear as she kissed my cheeks over and over. Then they were all doing it, hugging and kissing me. Escape was impossible. Then again, I wasn't sure escape was what I really wanted. I had missed them. All of them.

As we all took a seat in the family room, Dad switched on the television set. I concentrated on the first of two NFL games already underway. The Dallas Cowboys were playing the Miami Dolphins, and the Dolphins were circling the Cowboys with a 21–7 lead, two minutes before the end of the first half.

Papa Ray tapped my shoulder. I politely watched my grandfather's lips move. Then I looked at my Dad who translated. *How's school?*

"Good, Papa."

That was the start to a flood of questions that came from my grandparents. How were classes? What were the other kids like? Did I have a lot of friends? How was the dorm room?

I could feel embarrassment first as my cheeks grew hotter. My ears felt the heat next. I kept looking from grandparent to grandparent then to my father for an interpretation, nodding, and answering questions. Though sincere questions, I felt odd, out of place, like this was some weird interview.

Normally, when home for the weekends, I spent time with Mom, Dad, Marie, and Patrick. They signed. I felt comfortable around them. Never would I have expected to feel so strange and alone just because I was in a room full of hearing people.

I had to get out of there. When I got to my room, I realized my mother must have followed me.

What's wrong? she signed.

Finally ready to hear an honest answer, I found the courage to ask her something that had been bothering me for a long time. "How do I sound when I talk?" I shook my head. "I mean, am I pronouncing words right? Am I yelling? Whispering? I have no idea. I don't want to embarrass myself."

I'd heard deaf people talk as they sign. The words were more like moans, and difficult to understand.

You sound like you, she signed, and pointed a finger into the center of my chest. *Sometimes loud, but never yelling.*

"Would you tell me if I sounded hard to understand?" I said.

She nodded. *Of course.*

We sat there, side by side on my bed.

Are you coming down for dinner?

I nodded and stood up. "I'm starving. Everything smells great." I tried to smile.

Mom took my shoulders and pulled me in for a hug. Part of me wanted to pull away. Most of me just let her hug me.

⚮

Dinner tasted fantastic. We started the meal with a big pan of Mom's lasagna. Lots of ricotta cheese and sausage. When Dad finished carving the turkey I enjoyed a drumstick along with a plateful of stuffing, cranberries, mashed and sweet potatoes. What I liked best was that everyone stayed busy eating. A question here, a question there, I didn't mind that. Maybe they got all of their questions out of the way before dinner—at least, I hoped that was the case.

That was, until Dad and Papa Ray got into a discussion I knew involved me. Papa Ray kept looking and pointing at me. Dad kept his hands near his face, as if he worried I might be able to lip-read.

What's going on? I signed to Marie.

Papa wants to ask you about baseball, she replied.

I watched for several more seconds, the details of the conversation lost on me. I could only imagine Dad trying to get Papa to drop the subject. I knew everyone else at the table knew what was going on, heard every word being said. And all of them acted like nothing was happening, just because they knew I couldn't hear what they were saying. It was crazy and wildly insulting.

I got abruptly to my feet. "What are you all talking about?" I knew I was talking loudly.

Baseball, Dad signed.

"What about it?"

Papa Ray wants to know if you plan to play next season, Dad said.

I couldn't look my grandfather in the eyes. Instead, I looked at the floor and signed, *I'm deaf, Papa. Deaf people don't play baseball.* I left the room. Let someone else translate for me, I thought. Let them see what it was like *not* to know what someone was saying. I was certain everyone would continue discussing me as they had before—only this time I really wouldn't be in the room.

Just as I turned to close my bedroom door, I saw Marie on my heels. *What?*

Can't I come in? she asked.

I want to be alone.

Marie frowned and turned around. I reached out and touched my sister. When she turned back to look at me with hopeful eyes, I invited her into the room and shut the door.

They talking about me? I asked.

Who knows? I left, too.

For what felt like several minutes we sat on the bed, neither one of us signing a word. *Mom and Dad are so sad,* she signed.

Because of me?

They miss having you home, Marie signed. *Do you want to come home?*

I missed being home when I was at school. I nodded.

So come home, she signed, as if easily solving the problem.

And go to the school here? I don't think so. I like my school.

But what about Mom and Dad? she signed.

You're really worried about them?

You just see them on weekends. When they drop you back off at school, they are a mess. We go to a deaf support group during the week. It is for people with someone deaf in the family.

You do? No one had told me about this. *Do you like it?*

Batavia is not a big town. I'd never imagined there could be more than just me who was deaf around here.

I like it. And I think it helps Mom and Dad a lot. They know they are not the only parents out there with a deaf child.

I couldn't picture what it would be like at a support meeting. Did all these families just sit around talking about their kids, how they used to be, compared with how they were now? I wondered what they said about me. *Did Mom or Dad ever ask you to ask me to come back home?*

No, Marie signed, shaking her head. *They'd kill me if they knew I was telling you this.*

Do you want me to come back home?

Marie let a tear roll down her cheek before brushing it away and answering. *I miss you.*

Sometimes I don't feel like I fit in here anymore.

Marie looked shocked, eyes open wide, her mouth shaped like an "O." Then her expression softened, her eyes becoming thoughtful slits, her lips melting into each other. *Is it that terrible?*

It's hard. I missed home more than I was letting on, but I also missed school. I didn't want to be away from home—but I did like RSD. I found myself after one day already missing Samantha, Brian, and even Kyle.

Does it make you sad? She asked.

Sometimes I felt sad, but not as much lately. *I'm doing all right*, I answered. And I meant it.

CHAPTER 37

Shivering, I opened my eyes. It took a moment before realizing I was home, in my bed, in my room. Where it should have felt normal, instead it just seemed weird. I stayed on my back and stared at the ceiling. Moonlight from the window lit the room. In the beams cast above, I noticed a swarm of something floating around, like the shadow of bugs. Snowflakes. It was snowing.

I jumped out of bed and ran to the window. Fresh snow covered the ground in a thin layer. Though I could still see blades of grass poking up from the dusting of snow, I knew by morning everything would be buried under a white blanket.

I knelt by the window and peered out.

Snow was silent. Before becoming deaf, I hadn't minded watching snow fall in silence. I stood up slowly and pressed my forehead against the glass.

Even though there was nothing to hear, and no one could hear it, that didn't make things better. The silence still frustrated me.

I turned angrily away and jumped into bed. I pulled the covers over my head and shut my eyes. Then I snapped them open and hurriedly lowered the blanket. I glanced at the window again. The snowflakes had already changed and were falling past the glass like thick, giant raindrops in a thunderstorm.

I used to sit on the couch in the living room and stare out the window watching and listening to thunderstorms with my mom. We'd count how long it was between the boom of thunder and the flash of lightning that lit the sky. We'd watch the rain splatter against the window.

Sometimes the thunder was so loud, I'd jump. I wasn't scared. Not really. Not with my mom there. Sometimes she'd jump, too. Then we'd look at each other and laugh.

Getting out of bed, I went back to the window. It was months until spring. I didn't want to think about the thunderstorms that I would never hear again. Not now.

Falling snow was quiet. Peaceful.

I went back to the window and knelt again. There was nothing to hear. The snow that had fallen before I'd become deaf had also been silent. I smiled, rested my elbows on the sill and my chin in my palms, and watched the snow cover the ground.

Chapter 38

January

yle woke me up around 3:00 a.m. He was holding his head and crying. His skin was red. *My ears,* he signed.

I got out of bed. I did the only thing I knew how to do. I placed the palm of my hand on his forehead. That was what my mom always did to me when I didn't feel well. He felt hot. I sat him down on the mattress, but had no idea what to do next. It was the middle of the night. I didn't know if anyone would be at the infirmary this late.

Wait here, I signed. I went down the hall to Norton's room. I switched on the light. It did nothing to stir him. I gently shook the DC awake. Norton popped up, gasping and scrambling away from me, as if I was a creature from a horror movie. It took Norton a moment to orient himself and regain his composure.

What's wrong?

Kyle has a high fever. His ears hurt.

Norton followed me back to the room. Kyle was lying down, curled into a ball, wrapped in my blankets. Norton touched his palm to Kyle's forehead and then looked at me. *Hot,* he signed. *Let's get him to the nurse. Stay with him. I'm going to go get dressed.*

I put on a pair of socks, my coat, and winter boots. Norton returned as I tied up my laces. We must have been a sight, dressed in pajama pants, T-shirts and winter gear.

Norton wrapped my blanket tightly around Kyle, picked up the bundle, and started out of the bedroom. I ran ahead down the hall and pushed open the door. A bitter winter wind heavily peppered with large falling snowflakes assaulted us. Inches had accumulated during the night. I stepped into the snow bank. My loosely tied laces did nothing to keep the snow from falling into my boots. It melted quickly and soaked through my socks. The wet cold stung my ankles.

The wind whipped around wildly, as if trying to prevent Norton and me from reaching help in Forrester Hall. I knew if I could hear, the wind would sound like some kind of deranged werewolf howling at the moon.

We pressed on, Norton struggling to carry Kyle's sixty-pound frame. Norton trudged through the snowdrifts and snow banks, careful not to lose his footing. I trotted ahead, pulling open the door to the building.

The infirmary was on the second level. Past the reception area, a row of empty beds with white linen stood lining one wall; ceiling-mounted curtains could separate each bed for privacy if necessary.

The woman at the desk had been reading a book. When she saw us, she inserted a bookmark and stood. She used sign language to communicate that she was the night nurse. She was pretty good at signing. I couldn't help wondering if she was deaf. *What's the matter with this little guy?* she asked. *How are you, Kyle?*

Sick, he signed. *Looks like I'll be here a lot, again.*

She smiled and led Norton to the first bed in the long row of unused beds. Norton set Kyle down.

His ears, I signed.

The nurse took his temperature. *We'll take good care of you, like always.*

Mom, Kyle signed. *I want my Mom.*

Could be an ear infection, the nurse signed. After giving him some pain reliever and a cup of water, Kyle settled down. She asked Kyle to remind her of his last name. Then she went to the computer and called up his student information from an electronic file. *Both of his parents are deaf,* she signed. She used the TTY to make a phone call to Kyle's family.

I turned my attention to Kyle. *You okay?*

Shaking his head up and down. *I want my mom.*

Norton sat on the bed next to Kyle and looked as if he might fall asleep sitting up.

The nurse returned. *Your parents live in Albany,* she signed. *That's pretty far from here. The weather outside is bad. I told your parents it looked like you might have an ear infection. The doctor will be here in a few hours. Okay?*

Kyle looked scared.

You stay here until the doctor shows up, the nurse signed. *I'll keep you company while you sleep.*

Kyle closed his eyes and cried.

Can I stay with him? I signed. Memories of times I'd been sick filled my head. I thought of my mother. She'd stay by my side, maybe press a cool cloth against my forehead, or just hold my hand. But she was there if I closed my eyes, and there whenever I opened them.

There's no need.

But I want to. At first, I wasn't even thinking about my last big fever… the one that robbed me of my hearing. Then I remembered waking up in the hospital bed. Mom's was the first face I saw.

Norton yawned. *I'd stay, but I can't leave the dorm unattended,* he signed.

I tapped Kyle on the arm. *I'll stay with you. I'll sleep in this bed next to you.*

You'll stay with me?

Yes, I signed.

With the lights on? Kyle signed.

Not a problem, the nurse signed. I smiled and nodded at Kyle. He offered up a weak smile in return.

We got comfortable in our temporary beds after Norton left. The nurse made sure we were all settled in before asking if we wanted the curtain pulled closed all the way. "Leave it open, just a little," I said.

Kyle waved his hand around to get my attention. When I turned to look at him, he signed, *Thank you.*

We're buddies, right? I signed, then squeezed his hand.

Brothers. Kyle closed his eyes.

I closed mine, too, but I couldn't sleep. Seeing Kyle so scared got to me. *God,* I thought, *God—I've never done this. Not sure I'm even doing it right. But I was hoping I could trouble you, just for a minute if you're not too busy. Can you do me a favor? Am I allowed to ask for favors? Will you take care of Kyle? Help his ear and everything, but also make sure he doesn't feel so scared and so alone?*

I swallowed. I opened my eyes to see if the nurse was looking at me. She couldn't know I'd been praying, but I felt odd, just the same. The nurse was nowhere in sight, so I closed my eyes and continued.

And God, if I can ask for one more favor? Can you keep an eye on me, as well? I guess I'm kind of scared, too. And I don't want to be. I want to be more like Samantha. Not like I want to be a girl, but, brave—I'd like to be brave like Samantha. And God? One more thing. Watch over Samantha, too? Thank you. Good night.

CHAPTER 39

package was delivered to the dormitory on Monday. Norton brought it up to me. *It's for you,* he signed.

Everyone at RSD, myself included, loved to receive mail. It made the week more enjoyable if a package arrived filled with home-baked chocolate chip cookies or a card with some cash in it or just a letter telling you how much you were loved and missed.

I saw that the package came from my grandparents. I tore at the brown paper wrapping. Inside I found a letter, a book, and a couple packs of baseball cards. I thought of my collection of cards at home. At one time, they had meant everything to me. I pulled open my sock drawer, dropped the packs of cards in, and shut the drawer. I sat back on the bed and read the letter:

Dear Marco,

I hope school is going well. Your grandmother and I think about you often. We can't wait for you and Marie to come back for an extended visit. I convinced your parents to think about doing so during spring break.

I want to apologize for upsetting you at Thanksgiving. When Grandma Joanne and I got back home, I felt very unhappy and useless, like there was nothing I could do or say to make things better.

I know that playing pro ball has always been your dream. I've been to enough of your baseball games to know you have genuine talent. I don't know if you want to hear all of this. I know now that thinking of baseball upsets you. That is why I've taken so long to write. I didn't want to risk upsetting you again.

Until a few weeks ago I didn't think there was anything I could do or say to make your hurt, your sense of loss, go away. That is an awful and powerless feeling for a grandparent to have.

I went to the library and did some research on famous deaf people—and there are a lot of them. There are pilots, actors, authors, inventors, artists like Louis Frisino. Did you know a deaf woman founded the Girl Scouts? I. King Jordan is deaf, and he is the president of a college.

But I also found out there are quite a few professional deaf athletes, like James "Deaf" Burke who was a famous boxer in the 19th century. Then there was a man they called Dummy Hoy. He was one of the greatest ballplayers around who started his career in the late 1800s and finished it in 1902. Of course, Dummy Hoy wasn't his real name. His real name was William Ellsworth Hoy. Never heard of him? I'm not surprised. For whatever reason, this man has not made it into the Baseball Hall of Fame, despite all the records he held. Did you know Hoy stole more than 600 bases in his career? It's true. And it was Hoy who prompted the "strike" sign in baseball that is a form of sign language when the umpire calls a strike.

The book I sent has more information on Hoy. And Hoy has his own website, as well. It appears that the deaf community has been lobbying to get Dummy Hoy inducted into the Hall of Fame for years. However, on August 2, 2003, he was inducted into the Cincinnati Reds Hall of Fame.

Curtis Pride is the other ballplayer I wanted to tell you about. Born deaf, he was determined to become a pro from the time he started T-ball, regardless of being deaf. He signed with the New York Mets in 1989, and then went on to play for Detroit, Boston, Atlanta, and the New York Yankees. My point, Marco, is that you can do it. You can do anything you want to do. Deaf or not. Remember that!

I'm always here.

Anyway, I hope you enjoy the book. I hope you are
not upset with me still from Thanksgiving. It might be
because I am an old man, but I can't understand, Marco,
why you have to give up playing baseball just because
you're deaf.

Love and Kisses,

Papa Ray & Grandma Joanne

I folded the letter back up and set it aside as I reached for the baseball
book. I didn't mean to make my grandfather feel bad at Thanksgiving. I
must have really hurt him when I left the table. I hadn't really been angry
at him. Before the end of the day, I intended to write him back and tell him
so. What was there to be mad at? More and more I was accepting the truth.

I was deaf.

I knew that Papa Ray loved baseball and passed that love down to my
dad, who in turn, shared his love for the game with me. Some of my best
memories were of all of us going to see a game together. It never mattered if
our home team won. We just wanted to see a good game—some cool plays,
some balls hit over the fence and out of the park.

The book he'd sent about Hoy wasn't that thick, only a couple hundred
pages with a few illustrated drawings of the ballplayer. I opened it up and
looked at the summary on the inside flap. It said that Hoy began playing
ball in 1886. When up to bat, he asked if the third base coach could signal
strikes and balls for him. He was deaf and couldn't hear the umpire calling
the pitches. On May 1, 1901, Hoy hit the first grand slam in the newly formed
American League. Hoy died in 1961 at the age of 99.

I thought the book might be interesting, but closed it for now, sticking
the letter from Papa Ray between the pages. Hoy's career took place around
the turn of the last century. Baseball was a different game nowadays. It had to
be. It was more intense, and the athletes were better. Faster, stronger, bigger.
Still, I was going to read more about Hoy and Curtis Pride.

I had assumed a deaf player would be hard-pressed to even get a tryout
with a major team. Maybe I was wrong. Papa Ray said something about a
deaf pilot? How cool was that? I never thought about acting before, or art,
or flying. I suddenly had so many options.

Then I realized that people like Hoy and Pride had to be different than
me; they must have been better. As a hearing ballplayer, I was pretty good,

but as a deaf one with buzzing in my ears, and a cane, how could I ever beat out the competition?

No, the best thing to do with my dream was to crumple it up and throw it away. Start thinking about something else, about taking some new direction. I nodded to myself. It didn't seem as awful as I suspected it might feel—giving up a dream.

Maybe there were more dreams out there waiting for me. I just had to dream them up. Maybe Samantha would teach me to paint.

Nah. That wouldn't work. I even struggled to draw straight lines using a ruler.

Abstract art might work. Then straight lines wouldn't matter.

God, it's me again. Hey, look. You know how much I love baseball, right? Well, I do. I love it. And I think I had a shot at playing for the Yankees in a few years. Maybe not some starting pitcher, but I'd be in the roster somewhere. But I'm deaf now. So if I'm not supposed to be a baseball player, then I've got to ask you, what am I supposed to do with my life?

CHAPTER 40

MARCH

I found the RSD newsletter in my personal mailbox along with some other mail. I gathered it up and stuck it into my backpack. I had so much homework, not even receiving mail could lighten my mood. Teachers seemed to think I was only in their class. Why else would they decide to shovel out so much to do in one night?

I knew that getting as much of the homework done before dinner would leave me that much less to do afterward. Brian, Samantha, and I planned to eat together before heading over to the library. I looked forward to spending time with them. We all liked our study group since it beat doing homework alone.

The winter, like a vengeful beast, didn't wish to relinquish its hold on the season. If not for the words "First Day of Spring" on the calendar, it could have very well been January 21st. The snow stood knee-deep where paths hadn't been shoveled along the combination of walkways leading from building to building. Outside, though, the sky looked as blue as any sky on a given mid-spring day. However, the air was crisp and cold. Thankfully, the wind wasn't blowing. My breath plumed in front of my face and then vanished until I exhaled again.

The snowball seemed to come out of nowhere. It missed me by several feet before burying itself in a snow bank. Turning, I expected to see Samantha, Brian or even Kyle who was back on his feet after taking a few weeks to recover.

Eiji smiled, bent forward, and scooped together two handfuls of snow, packed them into a ball and prepared to throw it, all the while staring at me. I watched as the second snowball flew toward me, but it was too far to my left. In a sluggish manner, I shrugged my backpack off my shoulder and let it drop to the sidewalk. As I watched Eiji scramble to make a third snowball,

I crafted one of my own. I crunched the snow into a tight, hard ball. Eiji's fourth snowball whizzed past me, sailing a few feet over my head.

I took aim, ignoring the icy coldness of the snow in my bare hands, and whipped it with all my might. The snowball struck Eiji in the chest, knocking the boy backwards. Eiji lost his balance and fell butt first into a snowdrift. He got quickly to his feet and went right to work on another snowball. He had not learned his lesson.

I noticed a difference in Eiji's smile as he scooped enough snow to make a solid baseball-sized snowball. I let him throw first. The snowball he hurled fell short, disappearing into the snow a few feet from where I stood.

Winding up, I pitched my snowball, imagining it traveling at ninety miles an hour before it slammed square into Eiji's chest, exploding like a paintball against his coat, knocking the kid off balance a second time. Eiji's arms spun around like a goofy windmill. He did not fall down this time.

Throwing the snowball felt awesome; I hadn't lost my balance.

I shook my head from side to side in a slow, exaggerated motion, as if disappointed to see that Eiji still wanted to play. Actually, I was glad he wasn't quitting. I was enjoying myself and relished the opportunity to knock Eiji around with my snowballs. Eiji seemed to be enjoying himself, too.

Eiji was quick. He grabbed up snow, formed it, and threw the snowball while on the move. This one hit me in the arm. It was packed tightly, and though we were at least thirty feet away from each other, it stung when it hit my shoulder. It exploded into powder against my coat.

Unable to help myself, I laughed. I jumped into the snow, looking for cover. I made a snowball and whipped it toward Eiji. He dodged this one, doing a belly flop onto the accumulated snow.

I laughed some more. As Eiji slowly stood up, wiping the snow off his face, coat, and pants, I saw that he was laughing, too.

You got a good arm, Marco, he signed, using my sign name.

The comment almost shocked me. I smiled and shrugged. *You don't,* I signed. It was a cautious tease.

Eiji stared at me for a moment, before laughing at the reply. *I guess you're going to try out for pitcher on the team?* He walked toward me. *I'm thinking about going out for first base.*

What are you talking about? I picked up my backpack as he walked toward me.

The school team, Eiji signed. *We never had a baseball team before. Soccer and basketball, sure, but never a baseball team. The way you're always wearing that hat of yours, I guessed you play.* He rubbed his chest. *But after seeing you throw, I know you play.*

I don't have any idea what you're talking about. I felt tension knot itself into a pit in the bottom of my stomach.

It's in this month's newsletter, Eiji signed. *Believe it or not, tryouts are next Monday after classes.*

In the snow? I didn't know why I was surprised. That was when baseball season always started. Even last year, back when I could hear, we met on snowy diamonds for warm-ups and batting practice. Finding a white baseball in the snow was always fun, and usually allowed more than one base to be taken on any hit.

It's spring, isn't it? So are you trying out?

I don't think so. You were wrong. I don't play, I signed.

You never played baseball?

I used to. I don't play anymore. I thought about the book I'd received as a gift from Papa Ray.

Why not? You got a great arm. I could see you pitching no-hitters.

At one point, so could I. Long story.

Eiji patted me on the back. *Friends?* He held out his hand.

I shook it. *Friends. But I need to ask you something. Why were you so mad at me?*

Eiji's chest puffed, and then his shoulder deflated. It was quite a sigh. *You want to know, to really know?*

I do.

It's Samantha. I know she's your girlfriend, but I've had a crush on her since last year. I was going to tell her this year. Spent all summer working up the courage. Then you come to the school, and everything changes. But if you tell her this, I'll not only deny it, I'll pound you. We clear?

Crystal. But Eiji, she's not my girlfriend. I like her. She's cool. But we are not boyfriend and girlfriend, I signed.

Eiji smiled. It was small, but there was no doubt it was a smile. *You guys aren't dating?*

No.

He pursed his lips, as if saying *Hmmm.*

I know you've seen me with my dad? He signed.

I wasn't going to bring it up. Not now, anyway. Maybe sometime if we did become friends. *Yes,* I signed.

My older brother is in college at MIT. My dad is so clearly proud of him, but I think he's embarrassed of me. Not only am I bad at school, he signed, then laughed, *but I'm deaf. I'm a disappointment.*

I didn't know what to say. I wasn't sure why he was telling me so much. I tried not to make it even more uncomfortable for him.

My dad loves baseball, Eiji signed. *When I told him I was trying out for the team, he texted back that I should send him a schedule as soon as it's available. I don't know. Maybe that made him less disappointed?*

He looked at me like he wanted—or needed—me to agree with his reasoning. So I did. *That will be cool having him come to the games! Good luck at the tryouts.*

Thanks. And you should think it over. We might be pretty good together, Eiji signed, holding out his hand.

I was just going to shake it, but didn't. Instead, I showed him the special shake that Patrick and I used. Triple clap, up and over, and clap.

He smiled. We did it two more times, so he could get the hang of it. Then he punched me on the shoulder. Still smiling, he grabbed my coat as I stumbled backwards, losing my balance.

CHAPTER 41

amantha barged into Kyle's and my dorm room. I was on the bed, sitting against the headboard, the pillow over my lap.

What is wrong with you? She looked angry. Her hands were balled into fists when she stopped talking.

You're not supposed to be in here, I signed.

Tough. Where were you?

Here.

What about dinner and the library? she signed.

I wasn't in the mood to talk, and I sure wasn't in the mood to deal with Samantha's explosive attitude. *What's your problem? You're this mad because I forgot about meeting you guys for dinner?*

And what about going to the library?

Forgot about that, too, I answered.

She reached into my wastepaper basket. She pulled out a crumpled up copy of the school newsletter. *Did you forget about us, or did you just decide to blow us off?*

You have no idea what you're talking about. I stood up. I took the newsletter from her hands and threw it back into the garbage.

I ran into Eiji, she signed.

So?

So he told me you guys are good friends now.

I don't know about that.

Yeah, well, he thinks so, she signed. *And he also told me you weren't going out for the baseball team, even though you have a killer arm.*

He talks too much.

And you don't talk enough.

What's that supposed to mean? I signed. I didn't want to fight. I wanted Samantha to leave. I just wanted to be left alone.

Kyle walked into the room. *You're not supposed to be in here,* he signed.

Give us a minute, she signed, asking Kyle to leave.

It's his room, I signed.

Then let's go somewhere and talk.

Give us a minute, all right, Kyle? I signed.

Sure he signed, and left.

I want to know why you aren't planning to try out for the team, she signed.

I don't want to.

You don't want to, or you're scared to? She asked.

I'm not scared to try out. I know I'd make the team.

Cocky, much? But that's not what I meant. You may not be afraid of not making the team, but for some reason you're afraid to play.

That's not true, and you have no idea what you're talking about, I signed.

So tell me. Explain it to me, she signed.

There isn't anything to tell. I just don't want to play. Now please leave. I just want to be alone.

When it was clear she wasn't going to leave, I picked up the book from my grandfather, grabbed my coat, and left the room, closing the door behind me.

⌘

It rained.

Outside it was dark and cold.

I turned up the collar on my coat and braced myself against the sporadic cold winter wind that blew past me. The rain made the top layer of snow underfoot like a thin sheet of ice. If I wasn't slipping and sliding as I walked, I was cracking through the glass-like layer.

Standing behind the dormitory, I was confident no one would find me—if, in fact, anyone was looking.

That school flyer. That stupid school flyer. Things had been going all right. Everything seemed to be getting better.

But now this—a school baseball team—of all things.

I held the baseball book in my hands. I didn't risk opening it. The rain would ruin the pages. Instead, I stuffed it into my back pocket and pulled my coat over my waist to protect it.

I bent down, scooped out snow from beneath its crystal shell, and packed it into a perfectly sized baseball. Bringing up my knee, I locked my gaze on a particular brick in the building and pitched the ice-ball with all my strength.

I missed by three bricks—but kept my balance.

Come to think of it, I did pretty well in the snowball fight against Eiji. I was able to throw, run, and dive. My balance—or lack of balance—hadn't interfered at all.

The last time I really tried anything was before school, at home with the soccer ball. I mean, after that, and after trying to play catch with my dad, and after the baseball game with Patrick and Jordan, why keep trying? Why keep at something that wasn't going to work?

I packed another ice-ball in my palms, ignoring the cold, and welcoming the numbing sensation as I wound up. Again I focused on a brick and pitched.

Missing by one brick, I bent down and immediately made another ball. I thought about Eiji and his father. The tension.

I concentrated, imagined Patrick squatting, his mitt open wide, his other hand giving me finger signals between his thighs. I nodded *no* to the knuckleball and *no* to the slide. I agreed with his call for a fastball.

I pitched the ice-ball and knew even before it smacked and splattered against the brick I'd aimed for that I was right on target. I jumped into the air, raising my arms in victory!

CHAPTER 42

S aturday morning when I entered the kitchen, I knew immediately that something was up. Mom and Dad stared at me expectantly. Neither seemed interested in the full breakfast plates in front of them.

"What's going on?"

Sit down, Marco, Dad signed.

Finding my seat, I signed, *What is it?*

We just learned that your father's new health insurance will cover cochlear implant surgery, Mom signed.

New? I signed

Dad smiled. *You are looking at the newest manager. Got a raise, a better health insurance.*

I got back up and went and hugged my dad.

Do you know what that is? A cochlear implant? Mom signed.

I knew what the implant was. I nodded my head. *Some of the kids at school have them,* I signed. The artificial hearing device stimulates nerves inside the ear. The implant has a microphone that detects sound. The microphone sends the sound to a speech processor, like a mini-computer. The sound is coded and sent through the skin to the implant. Works like a hearing aid. Hearing isn't fully restored, but for someone who can't hear anything, it was pretty cool.

We wanted to talk to you about it, Dad signed. *We hadn't before because we didn't think we could ever afford it. It would have been too expensive, especially considering there are no guarantees with it.*

People talk about it in the deaf chat rooms on the Internet, I signed.

Then you know there are a lot of cons, aside from the obvious pros, Mom signed.

I know, I signed. The implant gets attached to a bone inside the skull. I had seen cases online where implants were installed and then became infected. So then there had to be a second surgery to take it out of the skull. For some patients, the implant just didn't work, so the doctors would have to go back into the skull to find out if something might be wrong with the equipment. I didn't know, a doctor cutting open my skull once... maybe. Twice? I wasn't thrilled about the idea.

I guess we want you to think about whether or not you're interested in exploring this, Dad signed. *Dr. Allen has given us some places to go to if you are interested. The process could take as long as a year before you get the surgery, that is, if that is what you decide you want.*

A year? I signed. It was a lifetime away if you thought about it. *I don't know what to do. What would you do?* I asked my parents.

Dad shook his head. *I can't say. I'm not in that situation.*

Me neither, Mom signed.

That was no help at all. The idea of hearing again or *possibly* hearing again should have made things easy. Instead, it made matters clouded and obscured. *Dad? Can we start the process with the implant and then if everything goes right, I can decide when the time comes?* I signed.

I wasn't surprised to see tears in my mother's eyes. I'd gotten pretty used to them since the summer. They meant she cared. How could I be annoyed with that?

You're getting to be so mature, Mom signed.

I rolled my eyes. *Not on purpose,* I signed. *I just need time to think about things.*

The next day, Sunday, we all went to church. Coming up the aisle alongside the pew we sat in, I saw nine-year-old Jessica Ketchum—the girl from my sister's class—being pushed in a wheelchair by her father.

After talking with Patrick back in September, I had asked my Mom about the accident. On a Saturday afternoon in September, Jessica and her mother were returning home from grocery shopping. A drunk driver ran a red light, smashing into the Ketchums' car. Jessica's mother, who had not been wearing a seat belt, was thrown through the front windshield and died. Jessica was trapped in the car for hours before rescue units were able to free her. Jessica's spine snapped. Doctors said she'd never walk again. The drunk driver walked away without a scratch, while Jessica lost her mother and the use of her legs all in the same instant.

Jessica said something to her father. They looked our way and waved. Her father wheeled her over. Marie and Jessica immediately launched into an animated conversation as my dad talked with her dad. My mother put an arm around my shoulder.

I watched Jessica talking: her lips moving, the smile. I saw no hint of resentment, or anger, or blame. And if anyone had the right to be angry, it was Jessica, even more so than I. It was hard to look away from her. She did not seem angry at all. If anything, she seemed hopeful.

And like me, here she was in church, ready to talk to God—perhaps hoping, too, to find some answers.

CHAPTER 43

APRIL

I looked out the dorm room window. The sky, filled with clouds, resembled an enormous gunmetal-gray battleship. The butterflies behaved like rabid bats in my stomach. I pulled open my sock drawer. I dug through rolled pairs until I found what I was looking for. The packs of baseball cards from my grandpa.

I tore them open, stuffing the sticks of chewing gum into my mouth. Chewing helped me concentrate, keeping my mind off feeling so anxious.

I quickly thumbed through the deck of Yankees baseball cards—the pitcher and catcher—an outfielder from the Red Sox, the second baseman for the Diamondbacks. *Not bad.* They would be a cool addition to my collection at home.

I opened the book from my grandfather and tucked the cards under the front flap.

Then I ran outside.

Standing on the front step of the dormitory, I scanned the area until I saw Samantha and Brian. They saw me and waved. I gave them a brief smile. I was relieved to see them. Not that it had been that long since I'd seen them last. Just an hour ago, I was going through soccer drills with them on the field to help them practice for their big game tomorrow. They had both made the team, and I liked to work on my balance by doing the drills with them. I had also discovered I wasn't a half-bad goalie.

I wasn't ready to head over. Part of me wanted to run back inside and vomit in the toilet. It might make me feel better. But I was out of time. If I needed to be sick, I'd have to do it now, out on the front step, off into the grass.

Then I saw Eiji, over by the side of the dormitory. The team uniform looked good. Dark blue and orange. We were Wildcats. No more Sally's Hair Salon. Only thing missing was my catcher and best friend.

Come on, Eiji signed, stressing his impatience with his tense jaw.

I took a deep breath and ran toward Eiji. We did the handshake I'd taught him. He really seemed to love it. *Your father coming?* I signed.

He never said if he could make it or not, Eiji signed, and laughed. *Doubt it. He'll be here when he has to be. To pick me up for the weekend.*

I found it hard to believe. I couldn't imagine what it would be like if my family didn't support me. *Why would you say something like that*, I signed. *He asked for the schedule, didn't he?*

Yes, he signed. *I don't think he believed me when I told him I was going to play baseball for the school. That is, not until I brought home the uniform last weekend. Do you know what he said to me then? He said, "I can't picture you doing anything other than getting into trouble." That's what he said.*

As we approached the diamond, I was surprised to see just how many people had shown up. The sight of the crowd stopped me. The stands surrounding the diamond were packed—just as they had been back when I played Little League for Batavia.

What is it? Eiji signed.

I saw Mom, Dad, and Marie. Who I didn't expect to see was Patrick and all of my grandparents. They all sat clustered in the first few rows of bleachers along the first-base line.

I swallowed hard to get the lump dislodged from my throat.

Samantha, Brian, and Kyle made their way over and stood next to us.

Good luck, Kyle signed. He hugged me tightly around the waist.

I mussed up his hair. *Thanks.*

Samantha kissed me on the cheek and then smiled. I had to admit, I liked it, but I cringed. I didn't want Eiji seeing the kiss, but was pretty sure he had. I chanced a look his way. He winked, gave me a thumbs up. I went back to breathing normally.

Brian playfully punched me in the arm. *Go get 'em*, he signed.

Samantha shook hands with Eiji. *Good luck, boys*, she signed.

Wait, I signed. *Eiji has something for you.*

I almost forgot, he signed and opened the bag he'd been carrying and pulled out an extra RSD baseball cap. *I got it from the coach.*

For me? she signed.

He put it on her head and then playfully tapped the bill. *Looks good.*

I love it, she signed. *Thank you.*

She took Kyle by the hand and, with Brian, they ran across the baseball diamond. I watched my parents spread out, making room for the three of them. Kyle sat on the bench next to Marie. Marie smiled at me from across the field. I smiled back.

My grandparents waved. They stood up, raised their arms, and twisted their hands back and forth real fast—the way deaf people clapped.

Patrick stood up, too. He held up his thumb.

I did the same as I walked out toward the pitcher's mound, Eiji at my side.

Then Patrick and my parents began to applaud, arms up, hands twisting back and forth. I wished Patrick could have been my catcher, like old times.

Looking more closely at everyone gathered, I saw Mrs. Campbell and Ms. Funnel. Dr. Stein stood behind the fence, behind home plate. I waved to them all.

Eiji slapped me on the back before he walked toward first base.

RSD was playing St. Mary's Middle School, a hearing school. They went undefeated last year.

As I waited for the first batter to step into the box, I looked around the field. My players were all talking to one another with ASL, making sure everyone was ready. They asked me if I was ready. I nodded at each of them.

I smiled and nodded at the catcher when the right pitch was offered.

A knuckleball. Strike one. A slider. Strike two. A curve ball. Strike three. One out.

I jumped in the air. I could do this. I was doing it. I shook my head to make sure it wasn't a dream. It felt like one—one I had given up on, almost walked completely away from.

When I looked at the bleachers, everyone had their hands in the air, waving them back and forth, bending them at the wrists. The silent applause was thunderous. I cherished it.

The second batter was a big boy. He looked like he might be seventeen instead of twelve. I waited for the signal, picked the pitch, and whipped it toward the catcher.

The batter swung and knocked out an infield pop fly.

The ball soared down the first-base line. I turned to watch Eiji back up and step past the line. It would be a foul ball, but Eiji didn't give up. As the ball came down, Eiji started falling backwards, his arm outstretched with his glove open.

The ball landed in his mitt as he hit the ground. He made the second out. He jumped to his feet holding the ball in his hand over his head and ran back to first base, ready to throw the ball back to me.

Eiji turned to look at the people in the bleachers, excited to see the crowd going wild.

His smile vanished.

I saw what caused Eiji's smile to drop. In the stands sat his father. The phone was still attached to the man's ear, but at least he looked at Eiji and gave his kid a thumbs-up signal.

Looking back, I saw Eiji casually wipe something out of his eye.

I left the tears in my eyes alone, deciding that I'd been fighting back my emotions for too long. Things were different now. I was deaf. But I was still Marco Lippa. That hadn't changed. Not at all. I still had dreams. I still had aspirations.

I had also learned that baseball was important, but it wasn't everything.

I looked at the catcher, waited for the right sign to be called. The batter looked like a hard-hitter by the way he'd taken a few practice swings before stepping up to the plate. I wasn't worried about being the best pitcher on the team. I wasn't worried about winning the game. I felt free, as if I had been released from a prison. I cared about playing the game. I was lucky to be playing the game. I knew I would do my best. What more could I expect from myself?

I wound up and released the pitch with all of my strength. The baseball flew like a rocket toward the catcher's mitt. The batter swung ...

THE END

ALSO FROM PHILLIP TOMASSO

Vaccination

Pulse of Evil

Convicted

Pigeon Drop

The Molech Prophecy

Adverse Impact

Johnny Blade

Third Ring

Tenth House

Mind Play

Fragments

o

COMING SOON FROM PHILLIP TOMASSO

Evacuation

Preservation

WWW.PHILLIPTOMASSO.COM

BIOGRAPHY FOR PHILLIP TOMASSO

Since 1995, Phillip Tomasso has had over 100 books, short stories and articles published. *Sounds of Silence* is his eleventh published novel. His thrillers *Johnny Blade* and *Adverse Impact* won awards in 2002 and 2005. In 2004 and 2005, writing as Grant R. Philips, Tomasso had two books for kids published *(King Gauthier & the Little Dragon Slayer* and *Jay Walker: The Case of the Missing Action Figure).* In 2007, his first Christian suspense novel, *The Molech Prophecy*, was released under the pen name, Thomas Phillips. Working full time as a Fire/EMS Dispatcher for 911, Tomasso lives in Rochester, New York with his three children. In what little spare time he can scrape up, Tomasso enjoys reading, B horror films, and playing guitar. Feel free to connect with him on Facebook, Twitter, or through his website, www.philliptomasso.com.

ABOUT
BARKING RAIN PRESS

Did you know that six media conglomerates publish eighty percent of the books in the United States? As the publishing industry continues to contract, opportunities for emerging and mid-career authors are drying up. Who will write the literature of the twenty-first century if just a handful of profit-focused corporations are left to decide who—and what—is worthy of publication?

Barking Rain Press is dedicated to the creation and promotion of thoughtful and imaginative contemporary literature, which we believe is essential to a vital and diverse culture. As a nonprofit organization, Barking Rain Press is an independent publisher that seeks to cultivate relationships with new and mid-career writers over time, to be thorough in the editorial process, and to make the publishing process an experience that will add to an author's development—and ultimately enhance our literary heritage.

In selecting new titles for publication, Barking Rain Press considers authors at all points in their careers. Our goal is to support the development of emerging and mid-career authors—not just single books—as we know from experience that a writer's audience is cultivated over the course of several books.

Support for these efforts comes primarily from the sale of our publications; we also hope to attract grant funding and private donations. Whether you are a reader or a writer, we invite you to take a stand for independent publishing and become more involved with Barking Rain Press. With your support, we can make sure that talented writers thrive, and that their books reach the hands of spirited, curious readers. Find out more at our website.

Barking Rain Press

WWW.BARKINGRAINPRESS.ORG

ALSO FROM BARKING RAIN PRESS

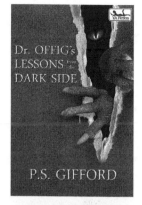

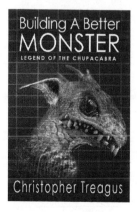

READ 4 CHAPTERS OF EACH BOOK AT OUR WEBSITE